The
ADVENTURE
of
ATTACK
of the
PYRAMID

BY
JEFFREY GARLAND

authorHOUSE

AuthorHouse™
1663 Liberty Drive
Bloomington, IN 47403
www.authorhouse.com
Phone: 833-262-8899

This is a work of fiction. All of the characters, names, incidents, organizations, and dialogue in this novel are either the products of the author's imagination or are used fictitiously.

Published by AuthorHouse 01/05/2023

ISBN: 978-1-6655-1110-0 (sc)
ISBN: 978-1-6655-1108-7 (hc)
ISBN: 978-1-6655-1109-4 (e)

Library of Congress Control Number: 2020924931

Print information available on the last page.

This book is printed on acid-free paper.

Because of the dynamic nature of the Internet, any web addresses or links contained in this book may have changed since publication and may no longer be valid. The views expressed in this work are solely those of the author and do not necessarily reflect the views of the publisher, and the publisher hereby disclaims any responsibility for them.

[IT WAS ONE DISMAL MORNING. The rain was bouncing off the copper roof, pattering as I listened. I watched the rain feed the gutters and just plopped down into my chair and listened. I walked down into the cellar and found the jar of pasta sauce I canned last month. It was so very tasty with big chunks of tomatoes flavored with sprigs of basil and freshly minced garlic. Then, I could see the lightning rod vibrate and twitch about, my house was just struck by lightning, a cobweb of white and yellow streaks. Then came the thunderous thunderclap vibrating the whole house with its sonic boom. The hair on my arms and neck stood up on ends. I went back to my chair. The rain would not stop beating, so I am joining in banging my feet on the floor. I wish I could be part of an adventure. That would do it; I wish I had an adventure. I am so bored I thought. I am going to go around the bend without anything enjoyable to do besides beating my feet on the floor. I turned on my stereo and I put on '19th Nervous Breakdown' by the Rolling Stones. Yea.

There was even a much more dramatic, and devastating, boom of electricity surging through the lightning rod. The house shook again, but the thunderclap was immediate, so the lightning is right over my head now. Sorry Mick, back to sleep. My stereo is grounded but with burst of electricity this close, I am not going to chance it. It scared the shit out of me. I straightened up from a good falling down. I had my fists balled up, since I was going bonkers; around the bend and wished for a fight in an adventure.

I wondered the house and found my chair. The kitty meowed while cowering under the sofa, the hound dog howled as a werewolf would to the moon, the chandelier began to chime from the rattling ceiling. I'm not completely bonkers you know. I heard a creaking and I looked as the basement door opened gradually on its own. Mist was rising from the floor and as the door opened, the floor began opening as well. It had hues of orange and red like the gates of hell just opened. So, maybe I am a little insane. The chair tilted me forward ejecting towards the opening. I could, faintly see through, there is fire, gases, and smoke. I see a pyramid-shaped statue or something in the mist of my mind. It appears to be the earliest of times of

Anno Domini, but the pyramid is vastly older. It looks like the Pyramids of Giza in Egypt however it gleams of polished gold. This all is like being in a funhouse, but this funhouse is rather scary, and not much fun. I fell into a room I had never seen before, old-fashioned furniture restored to new. I looked outside and everything is dirt. I can see the Roman armies leaving England or wherever we are? Roman, where am I, when am I? I remembered the similarities of the old movies. I complained about time seeming to stand still and now I am moving backward. What will I do without a stereo and phone? I do not care about phone calls. I could visualize the forms of others near me. Avalanches of fire cascaded in front of our bodies as we just stood in awe. There were four others there with me just as startled as I am. No one could express their emotions as we were all physically and mentally drained. We were surrounded by this cloud-like mist. It was wet, cold, and evil-looking. I looked again and recognized them.]

Steve turned to Stacy "What, did you hear the song 19th Nervous Breakdown by the Rolling Stones? '... You better stop, and look around, Here it comes...'"

Stacy said "Why yes I did. I was drinking beer and whiskey and just getting into the song when I ended up flat on my ass here."

[There are vast numbers of beings, I cannot make them out, visible in the flames which do not appear to harm them.]

"What are they?" Inquired Steve

"I don't know, but I believe they are just passing through." I spoke

Stacy commented "Who gives a shit, I'm dirty; I don't like being dirty. I want some whiskey - my ass hurts."

[We fell right into someone's sitting room in the distant past.]

"Hey Steve, what are you doing here? I haven't seen you in ages. And Stacy, it has been a while. Hi Amelia. Oh my God, Lisa! What a lovely sight you are. I have missed you so very much! I wish we would have stayed in contact." I stated

"What are you looking for boy?" Asked Mr. Ferguson

I replied, "A fight! Not with you, but with someone or something. You see, I am on an adventure. And fights are ensnared in adventures."

"You know 'they' circle and fester until they have picked out their adversary. An adventure, the fights and enemies do." Said Mr. Ferguson.

"You know, Mr. Ferguson is a bit too eccentric for me." Stated Amelia

"Why, because he can probably spell his name?" I inquired

I said, "You mind you and maybe we can all mind the other

things together, like what the hell is going on right now. Right now, we need all the help we can muster and need to work together."

"I thought it was all the help I can mustard." Amelia responded

"Shut up, Amelia." We shouted as one

"Bullshit, and I mean it. This whole thing is bullshit. I was having so much fun in my new Beamer and..." Infringed Amelia

I explained to Mr. Ferguson "We are from the 21st Century. We don't know how we got here, and we are just waiting to get home after an adventure and a fight. The bigger the better. But we are lost and do not understand our surroundings."

Mr. Ferguson told us that "Just before you folks appeared, I heard the word 'Adventure' and that is where it always begins – at the <u>beginning</u>. You see, an adventure can be good, bad, odd, pleasant and/or awful depending on what you wish for. The problem is that things never turn out as how they were wished to – that is where the adventure part comes into play; that is the unknow. Did anyone wish for a good or pleasant or scary adventure? Your wish came true, but how will it take form? Fasten your ties boys and girls because you have already begun what you wished for. 5 different imaginative minds wishing for different adventures but comes together as one. That has the making of one heck of an adventure, an amalgamate. Different thoughts may protrude at any time. This is *the* 6^(th) Century, 599AD as a matter of fact, and you are a long way from home."

"Have any of you seen a golden pyramid?" He asked

"Yes, I have just seen one as I was being transported here." I spoke

"Was there anything with it?" He questioned

"Yes, there were a lot of things, some kind of beings, but I could not make them out through the dense fog and flames, marching with the pyramid. Some of them looked like giant cats and others had a human-like form, but inhuman at the same time." I added

"Well, that is probably your adversary. We were too small in numbers to be consequential to them, so they just kept marching. But if your adventure includes this adversary, we will need a lot of help." Said Mr. Ferguson

[Mr. Ferguson was told a pyramid was coming. He instructed us to stay put while he makes some arrangements. He rode over to the Roman troops, but they won't fight any longer as they are ordered back to Rome. He tracked down the remaining English troops and many will fight in fear of another army starting another war while many of our chaps just want to go home to their families, homes and memories. Eventually, he returned with Clansmen from Ireland, Highlanders of Scotland, and English soldiers, all willing to fight again.]

Mr. Ferguson stood and exclaimed "We should do battle before I lose anymore crops! Besides, who can do battle if there is dust everywhere blocking our view."

[Amelia wants her car, Stacy's ass hurts and is dirty, and Mr. Ferguson is worried about dust outside. Am I just missing something? At least Lisa and Steve seem stable.]

I explained "This may be an advantage just like real soldiers. They fight covertly. And I know from street fights to do whatever is necessary to win."

[While he is gone, a pyramid and thousands of troops passed by his village. The pyramid is massive. The troops are a mix of hideous creatures. Mean, ferocious creatures. We are in awe because we have never seen anything like this in person. There are man-like creatures with them and some ogres too. It's like watching the circus freak show pass through town and someone left the doors open.]

I asked "Do you, Mr. Ferguson, have other friends that will fight with us? We are grossly outnumbered judging by what we have seen thus far, including the possible multitudes in the pyramid. We have only seen glimpses of their numbers and abilities which makes us susceptible to all sorts of hazards."

[Mr. Ferguson first instructs us to arm ourselves and offers some rudimentary weapons. I picked up a staff, sword and a dagger, Amelia and Stacy each pick up a bow and bag of arrows and Steve a long sword and a dagger, then Lisa a bow and a sword. Mr. Ferguson explains we must next recruit help from other villages as well as other lands since everyone here in this village is elderly. If they are all elderly, we must take the battle down the road to protect them from collateral damage.]

"Mr. Ferguson, has anyone seen this pyramid we speak of?" I inquired

"No, not until now. Before there were just rumors, but no one has claimed to have seen it, well except the local drunkard idiots." Said Mr. Ferguson

"What about the types of creatures we have seen?" Steve asked

"No, although I know of people who have spent their lives as scouts for the English army. They should know or at least give information on who to query. The rumors indicate that someone has, right? I believe someone has to have." Mr. Ferguson replied

I suggested "Hey, let's fortify ourselves first or this adventure will be over before it starts. Let us put the English and their cavalry on top of that hill with the cavalry on the other side out of sight. We will have the sun at our backs and in their eyes. We will have an elevated position to tire them as they charge. The others will line up next to them."

Steve said "I know what you are planning; that is a great idea."

Lisa asked "You are going to use ideas from movies?"

I said "Whatever it takes, remember. I will implore any ideas so we can win."

I asked "Have you watched movies? They have tons of ideas and we can apply them here. We want our soldiers to charge downhill, the sun should be to our backs, with 1 group of the cavalry to back them up. And 2 companies of archers to begin the battle."

"Bring them on." Yelled Steve "Sounds like a great plan."

I said "Let's keep the rest in reserve for now and possibly flank if we need, so we can have them sneak around the bottom hill out of sight. All archers should be out in front."

[Mr. Ferguson listened to my ideas and agreed, although I am not sure he really understood until I explained it explicitly to the soldiers. After a couple of hours, there is movement over the horizon.]

"There is a hovering vehicle scouting out the battleground. It is overhead, so we don't know what it really looks like. This is the pyramid again. Hold steady everyone, they are attacking.

Archers, on my command, ready your arrows! Target the ground troops."

[There are soldiers fast-walking towards us, but they look odd. Some are huge while the majority are just a bit bigger than our size. They pick up their pace.]

"Fire a volley, then ready a second." I commanded

[We are right in the center of the attack. While there is some damage done, the larger creatures are unaffected. The ogres will be tough to bring down.]

I directed "Fire at will! Charge!"

[There is clanking of metal meeting metal and then a thunderclap. There are several lightning strikes hitting our men directly coming from the pyramid. Their weapons are lightning bolts? What the hell? The large creatures are ogres, snarling, and swinging clubs about. We can only harm them with arrows, they do die, but it takes several for each. And then, out of nowhere, appears the pyramid. It has circled around our position; this isn't good at all. It begins to shoot lightning at us as well. We are being cut in half. The only thing saving us right now is the sun in their eyes. Unable to shoot accurately and the bright sun light gives us a chance to retreat and before the flanking army commits. The pyramid lets out a screech, almost bird-like, which sounds their retreat.]

"And damn, we had them right where we wanted them." Said Amelia

"Yea right!? Did you want them to decimate us before we fight or after?" I replied

"What the hell is up with that screech, and those monsters?" Stacy asked

"And why were we the only ones hit by lightning? No monsters were hit, just our men." Lisa inquired

I stated "If you wanted to win, would you shoot your own men? Right now, we need to get organized once again; they may easily return. They did far more damage to us than we did to them. That was our first look at them and what a frightful view that was."

Steve said "Okay, I vote you call the shots since you have been on top of things so far. We may have got hit pretty bad but your organizing the first round saved us from much worse. We will follow your lead in battle or to do anything else. All agree?"

"Yeah." In unison "Mr. Ferguson?" He said "So far, I agree completely."

"Let's start by setting up a perimeter with troops and cavalry support in a horseshoe shape. The light seems to have a worse effect than I anticipated, so let's keep using that – it's free! Then I want 5 groups of 5 scouts each plus a rider in each group to report back if they spot trouble. So, front line troops, second line of archers and cavalry support. Agreed?" (I learned in management to state how to do something and then summarize it also repeating the message so they get it down and they confirm it.) I said

"Okay, but I am already sick of this shit. I don't even know why I'm here in the first place." Said Amelia

"I think God afforded you extra time to work on your nails, that is why." I spoke

"I have been wondering the same thing; we'll talk about that some more tonight. Right now, we must worry about self-preservation. I didn't really think they would attack us, and we would be on the offensive. We don't have to worry about finding them, they are right here. And that sucks for us. Mr. Ferguson, do you think any leaders of the armies would have a problem with us leading?" I asked

"Let's, you and I, meet with the leaders. I know of Generals McKellen from Scotland and Glen who originated here in Britain, and both seem to be honorable men." said Mr. Ferguson

"Sounds good, I need a better understanding of how they have been fighting, strategies, and so on. I will also work on our repour since we all have to work together to survive. In the meantime, let's get set up as I have described and send out the scouts."

Steve relayed "Okay Jeff, everyone seems to be in order per your requests. They are all standing by in their positions. What do we need do?"

"I need you to find us fresh mounts. Has everyone ridden before?" I asked

"Yeah, I have" Said Steve and Stacy

Lisa asked "Amelia?"

Amelia replied "Hell no, it has a mind of its own. And they are hairy and smelly."

Lisa said under her breath "And it is probably thinking I should be riding her, the slut."

"Okay, this should be humorous if nothing else." I commented

"Steve, could you lend a hand to Amelia and everyone get to know your new 'ride'." I said

"Okay Napoleon, but if I get any dirtier..." Warned Stacy

Amelia shouted "If I break my nails!"

"And you'll be as useless as you already are." Exclaimed Stacy

"Lisa? You have been really quiet this whole time; what's on your mind?" I asked

"Well Jeff, I want you to command. You have been doing really well so far. Without your direction we would all be dead.

I am just trying to get through this thing. I meant a romantic adventure and this is all very dangerous." Explained Lisa

I responded "Maybe you will not be let down with the romance-thing."

Lisa admitted "That would be lovely. Remember, you have to do whatever it takes."

[About 2 hours later, the first rider returned a report.]

He reported "The general said to tell you they have spotted the opposition. They are circled around the pyramid like circling the wagons. The ogres are spaced out with troops filling in the gaps. The pyramid is sitting on the ground with some lights pointed outward and shining, but nothing like the lightning. They are all sitting over that ridge and it took me about 15 minutes to ride here and report."

"So that is about 4 to 5 miles from here. What is your General's name soldier?" I asked

"General Devlin, sir." He replied

"Do you have any reports of numbers?" I asked

"Yes, sorry sir. They appear to have 10,000, but we are not sure about in surrounding areas – that is being scouted as we speak." The soldier reported

"Fine report sir. Return to your general and explain I have taken charge of the armies, per the requests of the others. We will keep the sun at our backs, so act accordingly – flow with the sun at your backs. This has blinded the first attack, and we hope it will have some bearing on any others. Go now sir, you have my leave." I said

I explain to the others "More reports of similar activity come and go. There does not appear to be any reinforcements in the surrounding areas. I need to know our numbers. The number of cavalries, soldiers, and weapons for each general and then total the columns. That is all you need to do besides not falling off your horse on the way out. Lisa, can you take care of putting together that report?"

"Why, because you need a secretary that is a girl?" She asked

"No, it is because you look, and I know you are, smart, accountable, and can count as a matter of fact. You have my full trust and attention." I said

"Okay, and thanks for that. I am sorry I concluded otherwise." She replied

"The generals should have all of this information, so all you need to do is write it down and report. Thank you, Lisa." I stated

"So, I need columns of cavalry, soldiers, generals, weapons, artillery" I said

[Lisa returns with her report.]

"Sir, we have a report of your troops under your command. Everyone was helpful and very accurate."

"Amelia, thanks for sitting there letting us do all the thinking. Your cooperation is appreciated." Steve spoke

Leaders	Ttl. Troops	Soldiers	Archers	Cavalry
Devlin	1,600	1,000	350	250
McGavin	400	200	50	150
Glen	350	200	50	100
McKellen	1,200	1,000	200	0
Totals	3,500	2,400	650	400

"They only have spears, swords, knives and bows with arrows. Sir, I can continue to make these reports if you wish." Lisa offered

"Yes, this is fine work. By all means continue with the reports." I stated

"And quit calling me sir. That is like calling a hound dog mister or Amelia lady. For me, your pick, Jeff or Jeffrey." I related

"I like the sounds of Jeffrey. Yes, Jeffrey it shall be." Lisa replied

"General Devlin reported circling the wagons. Does that make any sense to you?" I asked

"That's right, he did. No, it does not. I do not know what a wagon is." Mr. Ferguson said

"Wagons were not invented until the 1800s, so how does a general in the 6th Century know about circling wagons?" I asked

"That's why you are in charge Jeff; the headaches. In fact, I need more tequila to stop mine. I need to suck on a worm." Said Stacy

Steve said "Way too much information. A worm, really? Not a snake? Leaves me out."

Amelia noticed "Has anyone seen a prettier day?"

"Amelia, we are surrounded by dead soldiers. Soldiers that died protecting us and that's *pretty*? Have some respect. Come on in out of left field for a while." I snarled back.

"How about, have some brains..." Stated Stacy

"So next on our agenda is to prepare for nightfall. They know we are here, I think, so campfires are alright with me. We need to start cutting wood for huge bonfires. If light hurts them during the day then bonfires at night should help foil their night vision. Let's get some wood Amelia. And then you can have some tequila Stacy." I directed

Stacy exclaims "Let's get cracking; or cutting. Whatever, get it done; I'm thirsty."

Amelia said "Yeah, some vodka would be good."

I added "Girls, I don't think you are going to like what they drink in this time so much. Steve, get some sleep. You have first night patrol. Mr. Ferguson, let's talk."

"Let's increase each group of scouts by adding 100 support troops, 25 being archers, and 20 cavalries to stay in the background out of sight leaving 2,500 in camp. They may be noticed easier, but we will have a surprising 1st wave of attack as they begin any fights they are planning." I spoke

Steve firmly said "Upon your request, this will be done as you command, your liege."

"Liege? Things seem really odd to me. I mean, besides us landing on your floor and the whole pyramid-thing. Do you have lightning bolts like that? And I have only seen beasts like that on Lord of the Rings or Day of the Dinosaur. Have you?" I asked

"Yeah, I saw Lord of the Rings. [chuckled Steve] "No, none that attacks people, pyramids I mean." He replied "So, what do you think about the wagon stuff?"

And I replied "The wagon has not yet been seen, but by us. However, carts have been around for many years I believe, so maybe circling carts was what he meant. I trust him so I don't believe they would lie about something so petty. Circling must mean you circle carts not our kind of wagons, but I don't know why you would circle carts really nor am I interested. Carts can

be of use to us though. I will waste no more thoughts of matter."

"It is too complicated for now, but maybe someday. Okay, so

beasts. Besides, we have enough to worry about. I do not want

to worry about a night attack, so here is what I suggest we do –

and please by all means speak up if you do not like something

because I do not know this time. I have had history classes and

seen movies about this time – by the way, movies are pictures

that move and seem life-like; however, I am not up to speed with

the accuracy or events besides the Romans returning home." I

added

"In fact, let's talk about this time. You said it was the year

599 of our Lord. That makes sense from what I have seen. Now,

we are from 2021 and very confused. Some more than others,

obviously. My senses tell me that Roman armies are leaving this

land. This is England, right?"

"Finally, yes this is England again." Said General Devlin "The

Roman outposts are leaving as well. You know, I think I want to

see a movie." He said

"Not right now, you old goat. In about 1,400 years maybe if

you live that long." I said jokingly [We both laugh.]

[Reports begin to come in from the company leaders. It

seems as though the pyramid is still stationary. Their troops are stationary as well. The counts are all around 8,000 with 10 ogres. Our forces number about 3,500, so number wise, over 2 to 1. Poor odds at best. They did have many more, so we are doing well. Someone gave me a count of 10,000 earlier but that must have been a mistake. It is really the pyramid that I am worried about. Its lightning show demonstrates their superiority alone. How do we battle that?]

"After that, we must get some sleep as I do not want Steve managing the night by himself, it is too long for watchful eyes. And the girls are too far out there..."

"Out where?" He asked

"Hello, we are right here." Hissed Stacy

"You called me Napoleon first dumb ass." I return fire

"Besides, it was Amelia..." She volleys back

I said "Out somewhere in the fog, their brains are besides here in reality." I explain "Too many focuses without enough brain cells to cover our bases."

"What are brain cells and bases?" Devlin asked inquisitively

"Never mind for now." I replied "Let's focus on tonight's plan for now. I want to change our fortification to a circular-shape instead of a horseshoe, so we do not have any blind spots. The cats could sneak in from behind. Keep them tight from front to back, so they aren't too weak. The main support should still be to our front and then count on troop movement reports to adjust. I want the generals to have their fastest riders ready-to-run given any movement. Each group of scouts will report to me before they locate their generals – I don't want any delays. Next, start building catapults tomorrow at the break of day. We need long-range defenses, or if things go well tomorrow, assault weaponry. What am I missing?" I asked "Oh, and we need reinforcements."

"Oh yeah, the other thing I am missing is what everyone was doing when they were pulled here. I was sitting around bored [reluctant to repeat I wanted an adventure] and all of the sudden a storm blew in and I was here." I reported

[Ditto and Ditto 2 came from the Boppsy twins. Lisa said she was hoping to add something exciting to her life. So, we were all bored and wanted an adventure.]

"Do any of you know about this time or what happens here during this time?" I asked

"No, except is this when King Arthur and his Knights of the Round Table lived and their adventures occurred?" Lisa asked

"Yeah and Guinevere ravages Sir Lancelot?" Amelia exclaimed

"Yes" Mr. Ferguson exclaimed "In fact, that all just happened last year." He added

"The land was not one without him, fell to ruins. The Romans occupied us and we were defenseless. Queen Guinevere gave him hope once again as she returned him Excalibur, the sword of power." Mr. Ferguson recalled

"What was more powerful, the Holy Grail or Excalibur?" Lisa asked

"Neither, as it was his return of love for the land and people that conquered evil and Morgana. At least that is how I learned as things played out. OK, enough for the bedtime stories or movies as you say. Get rest." stated Mr. Ferguson

I commented "And that is how a land should be ruled, love for the land and especially for the people. The land is vacant without the people and love binds them."

Lisa asked "And how do you propose that can be accomplished?

"Through love, kindness, respect, and honor." I replied

[Another rider comes into camp and reports no movement from the front. No campfires, no eating, no movement. That kind of puts me on edge as to whether they are planning to move or attack overnight. I relieved Steve at 3 am; he needed his sleep too. The only things he has seen were the reports coming in. I told him to be cautious with reports as the riders could be disguised in our uniforms.]

He said "Right, I had not thought of that. That could truly

happen. They could ride in and kill the leader, Kamikaze-like right?"

"Yeah, just like that." I said [what am I dealing with here?]

[I had planned a stealth night-raid. I had 10 assassins, 50 archers, and 50 cavalries with me. The opera Carmina Burana boomed in my head. I had the cavalry lunge forward and they quickly snatched the lives of many. We (me and some of McKellen's men) came in from behind and cavalierly took out one section of their circle. We were as silent as could be. We approached the pyramid, but it began to make a humming sound so we backed off. We managed to kill 2 ogres and about 50 – 60 soldiers, mostly beasts and some of the odd human-like creatures, without response. I could not get a good look at the pyramid since we were far away and risking too much in numbers. Besides, it was pitch black this night. All I could make out was that it was metallic, almost gold-like and just looked scary and powerful. We retreated stealth-like and pulled their dead in hopes of them not knowing. The ogres left marks that we could hide, but was still noticeable. If there was a morning reprisal, we would better understand their awareness. If not, I would be willing to bet that their only awareness was that of the pyramid. At 5 am, I readied the troops for a morning attack. We would have the sun at our backs as well as in their eyes.

At sun-rise, we charged in as they were preparing their own attack. We caught them off guard! The ogres clumped up in between us and the pyramid. I yelled: 'split the middle and flank from both sides!' We focused on the ogres. By this maneuver, we took away the advantage of the ogres' strength and could advance on the pyramid.]

So next, I yelled: "Full attack on the pyramid!"

[Arrows, rocks, swords no matter how big would not harm the thing, not even a scratch. I did have a Recon Unit in play – I organized after the night raid – that were specifically tasked with an assessment on the pyramid. If it wasn't for the night raid, I would not have thought of it nor tried it without its success. But anyway, we were ineffective with attacking the pyramid. Nothing we had could bring it harm.]

"Full retreat! Everybody back to camp!" I yelled

[Just as we started to retreat, the thing lit up and started firing lightning. This time, it was better with accuracy and it targeted cavalry first, which were able to maneuver quickly and avoid a lot of shots. We were able to escape with a few dead although many injuries. Their losses were large.]

I said "Let's rendezvous back at the camp. We will have a meeting with all leaders: us, the generals and Mr. Ferguson. Now go and spread the word we will meet at noon."

[As we were leaving, so did the pyramid flying up into the sky. I yelled to everyone, so they could watch. They took the things that kind of looked like men. I thought about going ahead and finishing off the ogres. Just as I was about to yell attack, the pyramid returned. It was unloading these odd, beastly creatures that twitched. I didn't like the looks of that. They are even scarier now than before. Come on, let's get back to camp.]

[So, we sat, introduced myself, staff, and Mr. Ferguson.] "Please, let's go around and introduce yourselves and noteworthy staff in your company at this time. Please with all due respect, give your numbers, weaponry, and any background about the threats of our opposition. Please hold any and all questions for me and my staff once we get through with introductions. This will be our first council meeting. Please start General Devlin."

"As you all know me by now, I am General Devlin, General of the 1st Brigade as appointed by our Lordship King Arthur. We number, after this morning's losses, about 1,500 with 450 archers and 200 cavalry. We have fought all over England. We will stop these beasts and things. We bloody-well better as we are worn on the idea of being occupied. Now the opposition I have only seen from afar. It seems that they only implement the pyramids when they are about to be defeated."

"I am General Glen and"

"Hey, he's an astronaut!" yelled out Stacy

"Let it go now Stacy," I said

The General goes on "What the hell is an astronaut? That sounds like a disgrace and I am a general missy. Mind your tongue. So, our numbers are about the same as General McGavin's without any knights. As far as the spinning thing you call a pyramid, we do not know. The only spinning things I have seen are empty bottles of scotch once its bin drunk. We have heard tales of it before, but never witnessed it first-hand. That was our first encounter and I thought only birds could fly. Is that witchcraft?"

"Hey, that reminds me of another movie with keyboards Encounter of the First Kind," said Steve. [God help me – give me strength].

"I am McKellan of the Clans. We r frum Scottlin' and have no knights but we r sneaky bastards birn to fight. We have no need for a general to be appointed or sired. We foller me. We number at 1,500 of the best swordsmen and archers to lay fut on the land. No cavalry, no horses, but we can ride. We still have more lads coming from the hills directly so make use of that.

"Hey, he's an astronaut!" Yelled out Stacy

"Let it go now Stacy. I think your whiskey is talking without an ample supply of brains."

"Thank you, gentlemen, one and all. To catch you up to speed, here is what we know. First, my name is Jeffrey. I have been appointed as leader. If there is anyone here who wishes to challenge me as leader, then let it be now so we may push forward. [pause] I have been chosen by majorities before to be a leader and I will not disappoint anyone except the enemy. The secret is creating a team, and you are that team. So, we all will be on our best behavior, not gnaw on the other, push forward to get the job done as a group, and no hero-shit with individuals as we are a team. In a team, you think more about others before thinking about yourself, and cover each other's backs. From what I have heard and seen so far, each of us has quite a lot to offer and we will combine our skills and teach each other to win this thing. We have a common goal and we will destroy it together as our individual parts will be insufficient. There are 5 of us summoned here by some force we do not yet understand. The reason for our summons is not understood. This has just happened. No one is to blame nor be held responsible. Our numbers are far outmatched. All we can do to remedy the situation is to fight smartly. If we do not, we may lose England and Scotland for good. You have been slaves to Rome for far too long to allow that to happen. We will fight by your side until death, if necessary. Now these tigers of a sort or whatever the opponents are, seem to be the main force. They are like big saber-tooth tigers with spiked tails. Our weapons are lethal to them, but they are very quick and agile, be cautious. That is why we must fight as a team, not individually, there are too many."

Amelia chimes in "Death? I didn't sign up for..."

"Shut up Amelia, he's on a roll, a good roll." Chimes Stacy. [Lisa tells them both to "Hush."]

Jeffrey continues "We do not have much to offer but knowledge."

"Yea, and hot bods." Amelia added

"Shut up both of you and put away the bottles. Actually, Jeffrey is wrong about this one as scotch was invented in about 500. So, there is plenty to drink when you run out. I doubt if either of you have tasted scotch before, but it is quite good. Then again, Jeffrey is pretty smart, so maybe I should not be explaining this to you. Please behave and let the man finish." Demanded Lisa "In total then, that gives us about: Tactician Lisa will report."

"OK, then Jeffrey, Generals and distinguished gentlemen/ladies [loosely], with those that have trickled in enhancing our numbers that sets us at:

✓ Soldiers of 2,900

✓ Archers at 750

✓ Cavalry of 475

✓ For a total of 3,125 in willing and able fighting men + 3 women. This is more than when we started.

Now the opponents are at about, per your reports:

✓ 7 freaking ogres, and

✓ 8,000 somethings, beasts, we do not understand."

"Has anyone seen archers or cavalry because I have only seen the soldiers and the stupid freaking ogres of the opponents?" Asked Lisa

"Thank you, Lisa, and to answer your question no. They may seem to be freaking ogres to everyone, but they kicked our asses each battle. I mean no disrespect, but they mean to harm us in the worst way. Those smaller humanistic sketchy dudes seem to be tenacious, but I think they only carry swords. So, for now, we should regard them all as fierce opponents each and every time we meet them on a battle ground. To be candid, I am worried more about those little 'freaky' creatures that do not seem to be human, although formed as humans. They are not human, just fierce little animals that can wield a weapon, but seem to rather bite our necks and heads off and slash you with swords. It's a good thing they are not bigger, although they too are bigger than any human." I surmised

I explained that "Each and every general are 'Members of General Council' and to instruct their men to follow the orders of another General in the absence of theirs. There must be someone in charge always. You will take charge as if you were a knight. It is in this manner that King Arthur of Camelot was successful in defeating the Saxons and we will defeat our enemy no matter how odd or inhuman they are to us. Our Round Table will consist of our 5 who were brought here plus the 4 generals who came to our aid and Mr. Ferguson if he is about. This is our vise that will pressure our opponents into defeat."

"So, how are the catapults building coming?" I asked

General Devlin explained "They are just beginning as we have already chopped down many trees in our vicinity for bonfires and then they are set back by this morning's raid. They should be up by tomorrow morning but ammunition is another issue. We will have to dispatch men to gather the rocks needed for ammunition. There are many rocks close by but they must be gathered right away to supply the catapults by morning. Then we can give them a fight." [The same reports and orders are agreed upon by all members of Council.]

"Then, we will press on from here until the next reports flow through. We may build carts for carrying the munitions, I can show you how if need be."

"Wait, what is a 'freaking' you speak of?" McGavin asked

"I, they". Remarked Amelia

"A freak is unnatural." I responded

"Is my Mother-in-Law a 'freaking' then?" General McGavin inquired

"Yes sir, if she is unnatural than yes."

"But she mothered my wife, is she also 'freaking'?"

McGavin said to Glen "My mother-in-law is freaking of the first order, I tremble."

"Meeting is adjourned" I declared

"These guys are like barbarians; I want one." Stated Amelia

"Shut up you whore-bag. Is that all you care about?" Asked Stacy

"Both of you all shut up you freaking whatevers. He just gave this great speech and all you can think about is who or what to hump. We could die here." Explained Lisa

"No, someone wants a boyfriend and it is not us..." said Amelia

"Just paint your nails, use the pretty blue pansies if you need to – although, I am assuming your nail polish is right next to your contraceptives that you left at home." Sasses Lisa

"Oh shit, that's right, and I won't even find a plastic baggie around here." Worried Stacy

Jeff said "Mr. Ferguson, I guess that did not go too badly for my 1st speech as a leader. I am not really used to this in these numbers. I kept thinking I am going to screw up."

"No not at all laddy, I thought it went very well. No generals left yet; nobody threw anything at you. Nobody exclaimed 'Monarchy,' and that is a good sign, so steady yourself boy as it only gets tougher from here. Cheers and chin up." Mr. Ferguson remarked

"So, Mr. Ferguson, I want a couple of things from you while everyone else is building our catapults and such. First, you need to find 5 strong horsemen to deliver this message to the soldiers. Next, we need to shorten our perimeter as written in the message carried by your horsemen. We may not have ample time if an attack should occur, so I want a smaller perimeter. We should have scouts spotting the scouts. With their numbers, they could take out an entire scouting post and then the next until they are on our doorstep. And for your final trick—you're going to be an old man someday, just kidding as you have already achieved that. I want you to find out how we can get additional information about these strange occurrences. You need to hand down this information, so future generations will have it. We are not here by chance nor are we just seemingly random persons arriving in your house for no reason. There is a purpose. Can you do that for me?" I inspired

"Why yes, I can do all of these things and happy to do so. You are right about the turn of events that seem inconsequential and the information is just a march away – wondered when you would get back to that. By your leave sir?" Mr. Ferguson replied "Old?"

[Next, I called in Steve from the ranks and explain what I have just asked from Mr. Ferguson and what I learned from our meeting. He agreed instantly and was more than willing to serve. I asked him about what he was doing yesterday before we arrived and he said he was simply bored and wanted an adventure like the rest of us. He was sword fighting with his little brother using sticks when we hit the floor. He went on to explain that from what he has seen and the orders I gave, made him loyal. As far as what he had seen regarding the pyramid, creatures, and ogres; this was right out of a storybook. I thanked him for his loyalty and offered the leader position over to him in which he reluctantly declined.]

"*No sir* Champion, you need to make the decisions if we are to live through this, whatever it is. And by the way, what is this?" Asked Steve

I said "I have no earthly idea and I use the term earthly loosely. Thank you for your loyalty. Now get some sleep because I don't know who to trust more than you standing guard come nightfall. And, I accept being Champion."

Steve then asked "Will you include me in the next night raid? I hate those bastards as much as you. I was kind of hurt when you attacked this morning without me."

I said "Well Steve, there are only 2, well 3 including Lisa, that I can truly count on and one of us has to sleep. When the timing is appropriate, you will lead in my stead. There is a great deal here to be accountable for and I could not sleep with you leading the first night. It is not a question of confidence, just timing."

"OK, I feel a lot better now that you have explained that."

I replied "For what it is worth Steve, I wish you were the leader – this shit is scary. Responsibility for others' lives sucks, it really sucks." I added

"Yeah, I guess it really would." Steve responded

[The fires are still burning. I sent out 25 archers and their guards for food. We have ample supplies for water. Our perimeter is sound. The men are building the catapults. Mr. Ferguson is seeking contacts for information. What is it that I am not thinking of? Should I be building defenses? What and how? From movies, I saw them making pongee sticks. OK, I can do that. If I do that, less men are going to be available for catapults. I saw once where guys were filling trenches with oil to burn. Still, less men on the catapults. I don't even know if the catapults will damage the pyramid. I know they would kill ogres and beasts and that is good enough. Yeah, they looked like beasts, so that is what we'll call them. So, what about this pyramid? The things I know about it are that it is metallic, but it may be made of gold. Back home. A nice Pina Colada, doubling up on the dark rum of course, on a warm afternoon sounds good. I guess I am where I was designed to be by God doing His will. My job is interpreting His will for me. Thy will be done.]

Just then, a rider comes in. He exclaims "Their formation has changed and they seem to be headed right for us! Should we sound a retreat for reinforcing our position?" Asked the sergeant

"Yeah sergeant, have your patrol link up with your general's forces and prepare to flank from the north. Rider of General Glen, ride to your general and have him link with General McGavin to reinforce the front lines as this seems to be a frontal assault. Rider of General McKellen, have his troops flank from the south and we will all meet in the middle for a victory dance. Make it so!" I commanded

"The orders shall be done as you command my lord." They replied in unison

[The wave is shocking. The ogres swinging their battle axes and clubs with veracity, blood spilling with every blow. The hordes of creatures fight with precise blinding of soldiers due to speed. No calvary, no archers, but just numbers and speed. As we barely hung on, the pyramid appeared over the ridge. It just seems to hover over the land. Lightning bolts shoot from each side taking our soldiers by surprise and vanquishing them into oblivion. We are defenseless, numberless, and without much warning. It was pure savagery. As quickly as the attack was upon us, it ceased! They just wandered back to their camp.]

I address the council "Okay so, they stopped just as quickly as when they started. They could have done a lot more damage, maybe wiped us out and they stopped. Why would they have stopped like that? Is this a warning? Why else would they do that? It must be just a warning. Does anyone else have any explanations, observations or conclusions?"

[The generals turned and looked at me as if I had something to do with the cessation. I was dumbfounded. I had no idea why the attack stopped nor would I have anyone believe it was me. I held up my staff and it was covered in black ink-like drawls, not red like blood – black. My sword is similar. This led me to the conclusion that they are aliens. Now how do I explain this to the others, and then to those of the 6th Century. First things first. I thought, I need another meeting with The Council. I called everyone to order.]

I began "Everyone in order... order, there will be no talking while I am talking. If you must speak or have something pertinent to add then raise your right hand and we will address you. Is that understood?"

"Yes, King Champion." bellowed by General Devlin

"I am not your King, my name is Jeffrey. If anyone does not agree to my terms, let them speak now. I can make room and accept champion but that is enough of praising me. [silence] As I was saying, let us begin with numbers and we will follow the order as our last meeting before this ghastly conflict."

General Devlin began with his reports "We have been reduced by about 150, losing 100 soldiers, 25 archers, and 25 cavalries. I think, I'm not really sure."

"Jeffrey, I have compiled the numbers here in a report for your review." Said Lisa

Leaders	Ttl. Troops	Soldiers	Archers	Cavalry
Devlin	1,300	700	350	150
McGavin	325	150	50	125
Glen	325	175	50	100
McKellen	1,400	1,200	200	0
Totals	3,350	2,225	650	375

I said "We only lost 150 men. That is much better than I had anticipated. And we still have more troops coming in all the time. Great job with that Generals. Alrighty then."

"Did anyone take a look at these beasts? They are like giant cats with 4 huge fangs and a spiked tail. I inspected a dead one. They also have huge claws, so carry spears and bows. Do not let them get close. Watch their spiked tails and fangs because they can use them as diversions. They are very fast and agile too. Keep your distance always. Use spears."

"Will you be staying with us after witnessing these attacks? We really need your leadership. We sould end up in chaos if you left." Asked General Devlin

I reply "Thank you gentlemen. Yes, I am staying. I am greatly honored by both your service and your losses. God be with those who have survived and who have lost their lives. We will hold a memorial service at noon. Let us remember, the service is for compassion of fellow soldiers and their friends in arms. Each of you will be given due time to prepare as your troops depend on your leadership and companionship if they should die. The next meeting will be at 2 pm to discuss the accomplishments of the catapults."

"Thank you, Lord – I mean Jeff." States Gen. Devlin "Sir, we need to call you something besides just Jeff." I reply: "May we honor you as 'Jeffrey our <u>Champion</u>' until we meet the King?"

"We will ensure your knighthood as we have already seen enough courage, honor and dignity our lord. And then you have the courage to carry forward." As all agreed

"General McKellen, please stand fast. I have asked you to stay behind for 2 reasons. First, you have suffered the greatest losses doing this battle and I wish to present you with these 100 hurses so that you are better mobilized. And secondly, I wish to hear some bagpipes playing at the memorial services today. I love tributes by bigpipe, don't you now? Is this acceptable to you?" I inquired "And a heavy glass of scotch to wish them well."

"Oh yes, my lord, I mean Champion, it would be a grateful honor to do as you request. And any other requests would be given in kind." Stated McKellen

I added "Fine then, let's get your men munted, besides a highlander munted is twice the advantage of an Englishman – don't tell anyone I said so or there will be anarchy again."

[It is 1 pm so I woke Steve while the girls are passed out and Lisa is sleeping. Steve jumps up and starts blabbering. Then he goes on about being in a hot tub with a bunch of girls and stuff. I explain to him where we are at. I explain to him how now I am 'Champion' and he gets a kick out of that as do I.] Next, I explain to him "We will be forming another night raid if everything else stays the same. It is now your watch and I am going to get some sleep. If the catapults are ready, and I hope they are, use them targeting the pyramid first. It seems like they take orders from it and that will give you the advantage. We must focus on the pyramid and destroy it." [He wants to tell me a story before I sleep. He started about seeing a movie when they used..." and I drifted off into a sleep.]

[I woke up and found Steve had everyone organized for the raid. I sat back and watched this time around. I started thinking and thought of 2 things. First, they did not finish us off today like they could have and secondly, they should either attack us or move on. Just then, Lisa came to check on me.]

"What's on your mind?" She inquired

"Well, I think we have something they are looking for or they would either have killed us all today or would not still be around. Maybe it's you." [As I tickled her just to hear her giggle and laugh.] "Seriously, maybe it is a goddess, like you. But this is killing me to see people die over what I should know. Do you know what I mean? For God's sake, and I am not hoping it comes down to another holy war, but what?" I asked

"Jeff the Champion [as she giggles], just look at the signs. We don't have anything holy here. We are just a bunch of people who are bored with our mundane lives and wanted an adventure and now we have one. Forget about the people who have died as they would have died anyway. They are still at war no matter if the Romans have left or not. What is next, I am not really sure but Britain tries to occupy the world, gets kicked out of the US, and then Germany tries to take over, then the US stomps the Nazis and so on. The point is that there is always a war somewhere and people die either for a greater cause or in vain. Which would you choose? The point further is that would you choose a greater good like us or opt for door #2 vanity. Let some pressure go man – I mean champion." She explained

I said "Thank you for just being you, Lisa. You really helped me relax, reboot, and be grateful for things as they will become your blessings."

"Like what?" She inquired

"Well, I am grateful for you and the tranquility you bring me." I added [I kissed her on the cheek, and she pulls me in for a real kiss]. "Love you more than I can express but I got to go. I just came up with an idea – you'll see. It's almost as explosive as you are." I replied

[So, I called in all of the troops. I called for a meeting with the generals.]

As I addressed the generals, I explained "I have an idea that is possible, but I cannot tell you where it came from. I need each of you to find good men to round up extinguished charcoal from fires and as much spinach as possible. Then we need Sulphur from springs. Rinse off the coals to remove all ash. Lay the charcoal, Sulphur and spinach next to the fires while making sure each gets as much sunlight as possible. We need to dry them all out <u>completely</u>. Next, we will grind them down into dust and mix them; it is extremely important to keep them all separate for now. I cannot stress enough that this mix will be very volatile. Explain to everyone just how volatile and deadly this substance will be – extremely. This substance becomes very explosive, so keep them from the fires and waters when grinding and mixing. Gentlemen/Guys/Girls, this will be gun powder or TNT! We will be testing and put on a display at noon today. I am hoping we can blow the shit out of our enemies, so no more lives will be lost, at least under our watch. With our catapults, (of which I have made with my grandchildren) we can have missiles, to a certain extent."

"What is shit?" Asked Gen. Devlin

"I do not have an answer for that sir, trust me, it will work to blow them up."

"Yeah, poop putty." Added Stacy so eloquently

"This takes a day and so does building the catapults.

Fortunately, there are no attacks. I decided against any further attacks until armaments are prepped and ready to rumble."

[No sooner do these thoughts cross my mind than does a rider coming in.]

He reports: "I am Joseph from Gen. Glen's division and I just witnessed, well I don't know what. I just know I am supposed to report to you, oh Champion."

"Well, what did you witness?" Snarled Amelia

"Well the thing you all call a pyramid just lifted up into the sky." Joe said

"Well, where did it go?" Asked Stacy

"Just up into the sky." Joseph added

"Is there any troop movement?" I inquired

"No, just the pyramid flied. I don't know where it went, I just knew it disappeared into the sky." Joseph remarked

"Well, what does that mean, it flied?" Stacy questioned

And I said "Well it flied, I mean flew out of sight, but most likely, it may beyond our sight and it will return. Hopefully, without a vengeance. Now let's get our shit together, or our poopy puddles, or however you put it, may shit the fan."

"Call all armies in except your scouts Joseph. I need your team to recon their position. I want to know all troop movements and especially, to notify me as quick as possible about the pyramid, if it returns and in what manner, as well as what changes occur upon its arrival. Can you get that done for me Joseph?"

"Yes, by your command, it will be done Champion of England." Joseph responded

Lisa said "Next, we have to find food."

I said "There are plenty of cats, we could fix Meow Chow Mein. That even sounds Asian."

[Still no reports of movements by our enemy. Evening has set in and food to be had. As does drink and a bit of partying, celebrating their fellow countrymen forgiving their lives in the sake of something good. I bought up Scotch from the farmers. We have bed down as well, for the night. Steve is at helm and I can try to rest a bit more.]

Joseph rides in another report "The pyramid flew back in and landed. There are no changes since when it took off. It doesn't look like it is hostile; it is just sitting there."

"No changes, it is just sitting there. Perfect, so the threat is no higher. Although it did return. That would be more perfect if it had not returned." I said "Why did it even take off; did it suspect another threat by us?" I inquired

[Out of nowhere, in walks Mr. Ferguson. This makes me wonder about why there was no forewarning of his return.]

"Guards, why has this man crossed our perimeter without notification?" I inquired

"Well, it is Mr. Ferguson and everyone knows his step." The guard replied

"So, Mr. Ferguson, what have you learned thus far?" I asked

"Sir, it is told that the pyramid has numbers of its own; up to 3 as I understand it. I did not find any eye witnesses, so this could all be conjecture. They come and go without much notice while it seems they command and transport 5,000 troops/cats each. Further, they are coordinated and organized. Each troop is foreign to our land and they eat their own dead, as well, as their opponents. They do not need fires or places to live as they feed on only the dead. And that is what I have learned in its entirety." Reported Mr. Ferguson

I reported back that "The current pyramid has left ground and has returned apparently empty. We are getting some shut eye for the night. I will explain more in the morning."

[At dawn, Mr. Ferguson and many have already risen, so we shall get underway.]

"Mr. Ferguson, we have developed a new weapon to use with our catapults that are now already for the next strike. Has anyone reported the return of the pyramid yet?" I asked

"No news has developed yet." Replied several

I said "Then prepare the ingredients as specified as drying the ingredients is of utmost importance. Let's test the catapults for range."

[The testing goes on for hours to be precise, well for rudimentary devices. We chiseled out rocks in which to insert the black powder in. We form fuses out of dried leaves and use hallowed stalks of wreathes. At noon, we will all meet for a display. We do not want to blow ourselves up, so an awesome display will prove or fizzle our hopes.]

[Noon.] "First, thank you all for your hard work. Unfortunately, these are hard times again. Will we endure?" [Roars from the crowded soldiers beating their swords against their shields and helmets.] As Moses championed God in freeing the slaves of Egypt, and let us stand as Jerimiah did in his fight while freeing the slaves of Jerusalem from the tyranny of Egypt, and Moses freed the Israelites, so shall all of you be set free. You were born free and will be freed again, as will your children be free for life. [I signal for the first blast which blows apart a portion of an unoccupied hillside as designed. The flash engulfs the hillside with intense flames followed by an immense boom.] If that doesn't put fear in their eyes, I'll dance a jig."

"Keep your dignity champion." Whispered by Lisa

[The crowd is silenced by the thunderous display of black powder. And then they roared.]

"And let us see the works of God and His son our Lord Jesus Christ to behold a new dawn. [A blast takes form in the sky as a bomb is catapulted into the noon sun. We are now ready for whatever awaits us under our protection. [The crowd roars with excitement and anticipation.] Let us take the battle to our oppressors!" I yelled

"Meeting with our Council in 1 hour." [Meeting at 1 pm with the 4 generals and my staff.] "Gentlemen, let's come to order. I have witnessed our display as a huge success."

"As was your speech my lord, I mean Champion!" Shouted Lisa

"So, let's take this fight to their doorstep. I want catapults moved into range in 2 hours' time. Next, we will fire upon them until there is nothing left. Imagine what King David did by slinging a single stone can be multiplied by what you have witnessed. Goliath fell to his knees with one stone and we have many. Multitudes more than one stone and a single sling." [All clapped happily.] Get everyone into play, for a full-frontal assault. I will have Steve in charge of armaments. The rest of you Generals will manage your troops as you see fit, but make sure our arms have quit firing because I do not want any more deaths."

"Steve, come here my man. The best range for accuracy is at about 100 yards, but use 125 yards if you must. Now they are noisy to move so getting that close is difficult. I would like to see 2 catapults launch and exploding into the sky to blind our opponents. Only then can we move the other 4 catapults into the fighters. After that, keep the 2 original catapults still and cover any retreat we may need. If in retreat, do not worry about the catapults as the cats cannot harm them. By the way, if I should die, you are in charge, Steve. Can you manage that sir?"

"Oh yes, Champion, and I thank you for the honor."

[2 pm] "We have the sun at our backs, men in front, and the firing begins in the middle. Let's not be shy about killing; we are here to defend our children. Allow for no quarter; none given, none taken, just fight to the last breath. Let's get 'em cowboys!"

"What is a cuwbuy?" General McKellen asks "Never mind for now; he's on a roll again." replies Amelia

[Crackles and booms in the sky. Lights as bright as the lightning begin. Then there is just dust from General Devlin's riders storming ahead. Then begins a barrage of thunderous booms taking out the ogres and soldiers. They lie burnt and dead all over the battlefield. A burnt hair stench abounds them. The rocks crush many beasts, they took a pounding]

[All of the sudden out of nowhere, the pyramid touches off and starts firing randomly. They target nothing, just random firing, or so it seems. Men begin to cry out and fall all around me. There is much despair. [Should we retreat or are they just frightened?]

"Full retreat! I yell without moments to calculate. We are just losing too many. And we were doing so very well in our fight. I was always taught that nobody likes a quitter, but that is for holding hand grenades and black powder too." Said Stacy

"That really is sensible. She should receive more credit, right? Not." I remarked

After everyone is back, I yelled out "Council Meeting in 1 hr. and get your numbers clear. Give me a 100 yd. perimeter. Make sure all catapults are back and keep making the ingredients for the 'black powder' and more catapults! Thank you, everyone, for your efforts." [I am really pissed. The morale was up, the men were fighting to their last breaths and the only thing to show for it is a beating. What a bitch that was!]

[Lisa comes over and tries to calm me down. Actually, she is the first I would expect to high-tail it and run, but she knows me.] She begins by stating the obvious "We would have won if it wasn't for that pyramid. They were just dancing with fire. We beat them. Remember your speech: Goliath fell to his knees. They did, the giants did fall. I beg of you to remember one thing; we are your family now. Like it or not, this is what you have. You planned, fought, and protected your family just as any human would – except you are better. You have something that many families do not have and that is love. Love for a better place, for a new beginning, and a power greater than ourselves. It's all about love. You have it, I've seen and heard you in action, love for everything around you that should be better than you can possibly be. Here now and relax."

[She laid my head on her lap, began to stroke a harp and sang:]

➤ I once was a girl from Nottingham,
➤ And then found out it was a naughty land,
➤ And then I met a Champion,
➤ A brave soul of our foundation,
➤ Who taught us to fight for freedom?

➤ Next our fighter Champion,
➤ Who fought only for freedom,
➤ Became bewildered as to freedom,

- He asked questions like how and why?
- Then felt his thoughts would die,
- Along with our freedom.

- Don't ask why for freedom,
- Or you would not be the champion,
- We all need your courage and strength,
- To find a new home for Kent,
- Then why did we need a Champion at all,
- We are the ones that would fall,
- And that is why we need our Champion.

[I fell to sleep as this song was comforting and her voice reassuring]

I woke up and jumped to my feet as General McKellen was there. "Explain yourself sir."

McKellen said "We picked out the perfect sword for you and a munt to get you uff yur feet man. Calm down sun. Yu alright with this?"

Yes sir, [as I wielded a fine, very fine sword indeed.] I thank you for your bearings of fine swordsmanship and impeccable horses. Yes, I am eternally grateful for your gifts. I am eternally grateful with your gifts and your abrupt awakening. We need to meet again in 1 hour." I endorsed

"Well ulrighty then as you say." McKellen returns

[1 hr. later, the Council meets.] "Alright, bring to order. We are all here and accounted for. First order is that Lisa is the official secretary, or scribe as you would call it, as she has been already taking notes and writing reports. Any opposition? Fine then, we want notes to pass down to future generations for accuracy and unravel questions. Back to the basics. We have killed a lot of beasts; which are the big cats. In a moment, I will again ask for your numbers. For now, my plans are simple: we need more catapults and black powder. Get your best men on it directly because tomorrow is too late. Next, I need your best men on it like in yesterday! I apologize for the abruptness; however, this means lives and I am not about to sacrifice more than what is already spent in this campaign."

I added "You have either participated or heard of the Christian Campaigns. We are the newest campaign and must act accordingly. Don't think, just do as we are in peril. Leave the thinking to me unless to challenge my authority. Action gets it done. I want to keep making the gunpowder, catapults, and collecting rocks for the catapults before there are any more raids on us. Abandon the harnesses. So, please tend to that fur nuw

General McKellen and the rest of you. Let's also round up more horses since their speed will help our attacks too. Has there been any reports of reinforcements yet?" I asked

"Nothing yet, but I am expecting to double my numbers." General McKellen disclosed

General Devlin added "We should be expecting another army of 1,000 fine fighting Brits I have learned. They have begun their march this morning, mate."

"Great news gentlemen." I said "Thank you all. Now let's get building and gathering. General McGavin please gather food and General Glen gather horses."

I walked off as Amelia grabs me and says "Another fine speech, but if Lisa put that in your head then piss-off, I don't want it, I don't need it, and I won't tolerate it. It is just you that I want. Even if I am wrong, and it is Stacy feeding you this shit, then I hope she dies in the next fight! I want *you* in the worst way, no bullshitting around."

"Enough of the bullshit Amelia, you just want what others have and I am willing to bet, it wasn't ever enough growing up, existing, nor getting what everyone else has. Did your parents bring you up poorly or is that someone else's fault too? Who needs what and who needs who?" As spoken by my examination "Let us get to the basics and leave others out of it. We are fighting for a population and not ourselves. Let me guess, you were just sitting around home wishing for what you did not have or wanted to meet a Knight in shining armor or whatever, just before hitting Mr. Ferguson's floor?" I asked

"Well, I love jewelry" she stated "OK, then get our group together." I exclaimed

"We'll get them together yourself, oh Champion."

"OK then, I will. And just for your information, I have only known you for a couple of days now, but I love you too. Just not romantically."

"Here is our numbers champion, we have gained some men coming in and they are fighting men also, basically replacing what we have lost so far, so I included them:"

Leaders	Ttl. Troops	Soldiers	Archers	Cavalry
Devlin	1,400	900	350	175
McGavin	400	200	50	150
Glen	400	200	100	100
McKellen	1,225	925	200	100
Totals	3,425	2,325	700	525

[So, we circle the Council and I begin abruptly.] "Were any of you thinking about something substantial before you were transported here? I know for myself; I was missing a gold watch. Anyone else?" I asked

"Yeah, I was thinking about my mom's silver necklace and should-be-mine gold earrings." Said Amelia

"So, besides wishing we had an adventure, we all were thinking about jewelry." I stated

"God, I forgot about my Mom's gold necklace." Wondered Lisa

And Stacy chimes in with "I was thinking about my bitch sister and her getting my grandmother's gold earrings."

"Besides the falling into Mr. Ferguson's floor, hoping or wishing for an adventure, seems to mean something about jewelry is common too."

[Lisa waits behind to taunt me about Amelia.] Then she asked "Had no kiss for little Amelia? The cute little puppy. Well, dog maybe. What could jewelry possibly mean?"

I reply "Have you heard of contact diseases? I don't know, I mean I have no idea. We all have jewelry that we cherish, but so does most people. Maybe it was the price for an adventure. Things will fit into place eventually. Until then, we have enough to worry about – like self-preservation. I need to get a nap, but don't let me sleep all day."

"OK, I'll just come with you for now. Maybe I can get some shut-eye too," Lisa suggested

"Oh, my champion... Okay, Sleeping Beauty; you have had your beauty sleep, time to get up! Shake it off and 'Stand To' ya bum! Here, I got you some grub. Guess what's on tonight's menu: steak! General McGavin found a small herd of cattle over the hill and they are carving them as we speak. I'll bet you are a rib-eye man? That is what I ordered for you. Oh, and do you want to hear something funny. Your 'Teacher's Pet' was over you in about 2 hours' time. She found some bough in Devlin's camp and follows him around like a poor lost kitten, which she is, except more of a dog in heat." Lisa informed me

"Thank you, Lord Jesus, that was a bundle of straws, more like a bail, that was about to break my back. Speaking of my back, can we get a few cots for the pathetic people of the 21st century? I am whining, I know; but you are the only one I can trust with my frailties. Everyone else must only see strength from me. By the way, did you get some sleep too? You look ravishing." I spoke

"Yeah, a few minutes. Ravishing?" Lisa replied

"Absolutely ravishing."

"That is all I had time for." Lisa said "Oh, and thank you my

Lord, I mean my 'Champion'. Ravishing from a Champion is quite an honor."

I said "Stop it. You do look as ravishing as the first time we met way back in college."

"So, you remember that? That was a long time ago." I said "Shut up, if you can remember. I am younger than you. Besides, you made a pretty huge impact on my life 'Big Sister'. Tall, blonde, sexy, long legs, smart, intelligent and an incredible laugh and sense of humor. The thing I remember most about the university is you. What a stunner as you are now. Yeah, of course I remember, I remember our talks and time together; and when you caught me with my shoes on the wrong feet, right? In fact, I think you laughed at me more than you talked to me. I guess I was a funny sight with my drunken escapades."

Lisa responded "Hey, do you know any of these other guys or girls, using the terms girls loosely?"

"Yeah, I remember a Steve, he was a close friend in high school, but looks only similar to my friend like how people change in a dream. I knew a Stacy, she used to go to the same bar as me. Amelia was like a slut I had for a girlfriend, but her name was different than Amelia and so were her looks. More pieces to the puzzle and thanks for that... Really though, thanks – I had not picked up on that yet. As to why I would know similar people from my past and them being part of this thing, I haven't a clue." I spoke

"First order of business: You need a bath. I laid down next to you and you stink. I will get you all lathered up. Then, we need another meeting." Lisa commanded

"You are perfectly right. Let's begin. Will you wash my toes for me, wench?" I inquired

"No, but I'll get you 2 bars of soap since you are really starting to stink!" She returned

[5 pm] "Let's get under way my Council. First order of business: Is there any troop activity from our opposition?" I inquired

Reported General Devlin "No Champion, I have had scouts overlooking their position all night and day – nothing. They seem to be just laying around almost dead. I would have attacked but not without your command sir."

"Any news on your reinforcements General? I inquired

"Yes sir, they will be in camp by midnight. There are 1,000 coming in with 200 archers and 250 cavalries." Stated General Devlin

General Glen reported: "We have 200 soldiers coming in to camp now."

General McKellen reported "We will have another 1,000 soldiers in camp by nightfall, 100 of which are cavalry trups.

There should be another 500 fut soldiers in camp by durk. We have runded up 200 herses for ur min."

"With those men coming in, we will have 5,550 men total and I'll finish a report after the Meeting." Lisa said

"Thank you, gentlemen, for your reports and loyalty. All of your leadership is greatly appreciated. I do not think we should venture another attack tonight, so let your men rest. I will still need to have outposts of about 50 men each, mainly archers and cavalry to assault if needed to slow advances. Now, let's prepare for a feast! You have earned it as do your troops." I recommended

[Night falls and men do come into camp gradually. Everyone seems to be in good spirits. Things are just not right, however. I cannot pin point why, but something is off. I ordered riders to check our outposts. Fortunately, all is well there also. Next, I order reinforcements to the outposts as we cannot be caught on our backs.]

[I call Steve and Lisa to my side.] "Summon the generals, quietly as I do not want to stress the men.] "Surry to stir up the purty," I said mimicking his Scottish accent

"You have Scot in yur blood mun." Suggested McKellen inquisitively

"Let's get down to it, so we can return to the party. First, does anyone have odd feelings right now? I feel off and I do not know why. My hair on my arms is standing straight up and that is enough for me. Put another way, I feel like I am in Mick's 99th floor flat looking out (Rolling Stones 'Get Off of My Cloud), helplessly – if anyone can relate?"

[Lisa and Steve may be the only ones who can relate, seriously. For now, let's protect our position. Have everyone break up the party, have half bed down and the other half re-enforce the outposts. I don't like this at all."

"It will be done as you request our Champion." Stated Steve

"And another thing," I added "Please call me Jeffrey in our meetings and 'Champion' in front of the men. It's a thing of acquaintance and comfortability."

[I feel I need to watch and observe for the night. I need to observe their camp, look for any weaknesses and potential feebleness.]

I decided "I need 100 archers who are sober to come with me while I observe. They have to be very quiet as the cats have keen senses usually. I want to observe first and possibly fire some arrows if the opportunity presents itself."

[Next, plops down Lisa.] "I guess you are wondering what happened with your alert; all is fine. Let's get out away from here for now. Then you can get back and be you're old Champion self again."

"Thanks for the invite, and it is a great one; but I have to observe, just overnight, for myself. Tomorrow, I'll do the same. If Devlin is right, we will initiate a day-raid. The light should help blind them and victory should be ours. But for now, what are they doing after dark. Do you remember the song "After Dark" by Tito and the Tarantulas? *...and the note says only after dark...* It might mean something [As it continued playing in my head.]. Besides, I cannot have others do what I am able to do for myself. They need reassurance of my getting into the trenches with them. Next, we need an air force, so if you know how to fly, let me know. Until then, we are grounded. Let's work on that, we are the best and have the 2 smartest minds in our neighborhood and we'll come up with something. What about hot air balloons or something? No, nothing to use for cloth I don't think."

"OK, 'till then my Champion!?" She replied

[So, I observe the rest of the evening and night. I decided we should cut back their numbers some. We fired 4 volleys into their masses and most of them hit their targets. We waited and no reprisal; they did not even try to attack. During the day, Devlin is right – they seem to lay dormant like to re-charge. At night, they are wild and full of juice. I guess the best odds are during sunlight. This is blinding to them taking away a major sense, well at least, to us. At night, I don't want to tangle with that savagery. Not quite yet, anyway. Now, with our re-enforcements, maybe another night raid is a good idea.]

"So, we have readied the catapults, their supplies of ammunition, and the renumeration; so, let's take the fight to them. Hell yea, let's pick our fight! It is now and it will be strong! Get the catapults, archers, and cavalry all in range. Soldiers will be on stand-by upon my command to attack. Let me know as soon as they are ready to rumble!" I directed

"Everything is into your specifications, just like you ordered. Except 'rumble,' what's that?" Asked General Glen

"I've got to get a dictionary for these guys." I said to Lisa

Lisa said, "Yea, and deodorant!" Lisa comments – "Yuk!"

"Let's get fighting..." I commanded "Open up with the catapults and fire! Let loose with the archers and pound their troops for a while! Steve, I want you to lead the ground assault. Generals, I want you to lead your calvary and General McKellen your fut suldiers. Attack when you hear 2 catapults crack at the same time. Steve, that is in 10 minutes time; they don't have watches yet. You are the time piece for them so be accurate. Launch the cavalry as the troops approach. Aim the catapults at the pyramid and fire!"

[A huge crack-boom fills the sky. The attack is on. The troops converge on the enemy. They lay dormant even with all that noise. The catapults lay siege on their position. They remain dormant. Maybe they are recharging or something. Let's take advantage of this by all means. We kill them by about 1,000 without movement. Then the pyramid starts to hum and raise. I sound a quick retreat. The beasts begin to stir and fight as we retreat. We get away fairly cleanly until the pyramid begins to fire. Again, no opponents are struck. Our losses range 1 of ours to every 50 of theirs. I can live with that.]

[Observation: The explosions have little effect on the pyramid physically, but effects its line of sight – the sunlight seems to do as much damage as it tries to lift off. Those gruesome punks are getting blown to smithereens though.]

"We'll see what our trups can du to them now thut we've stirred 'em up a bit." Said General McKellen

"Where do we go from here Champion?" Inquired Steve

I said "We will have another meeting in 1 hour." I directed "Steve, you will be timekeeper."

"Has anyone noticed anything different this go-round?" I asked

"Yes, they seem to be chaotic in the morning. Maybe they were at first too and we did not notice directly." General McGavin infused

"Yes, my observation as well. This gives us stronger hope and faith to do good." I inspired

"That is when we must plan our attacks as, they are too hyper at night to get a fresh jump. I don't want everyone to come running, except with fresh observations."

"Keep in mind, though, it is even the smallest things that may make all the difference in the world; so, keep them stored in your minds. We have to stay focused on saving lives – our troops first. Has anyone witnessed direct hits by the catapults? Has there been any damages further than the obvious?" I questioned

General Devlin reported "Yes, sure. Those little squirrels are looking pretty bewildered once they get hit. They are not organized, looking smart..."

"They have nev'r looked smurt so that is besides the pint." Insisted General McKellen

"Agreed, they are nothing without their coordination of the Mother Ship... oops" I added

"What is a Mother Ship? What is a ship doing out here in the forests? How would a ship maneuver on the ground? I do not understand." Inquired General McGavin.

"Well, that means they have sailed here from far off lands..."

"Stop, I apologize to all of you for me not being clearly spoken. I am sorry. It is pertinent that we are all clear about my questions, statements, and concerns to act as a team. A Mother Ship controls the others. That is all I have for now. Get your men some grub; shit yes Grubs are worms and I mean get them some food as it has been a tough day. Tend to wounds and rejuvenate the hope of your men. We need enthusiasm and ferver."

[The next thing I know are great reports. Many more men have come in as they have been. More troop re-enforcements are coming in and we now have a Wizard among them!]

"I am Jeffrey, Champion of this land. What say you, Wizard? Do you know of such things, what are their weaknesses? Speak freely now." I inquired

"Well, the troop re-enforcements are mine. My coming is that of my own. We have battled these beasts before and never wished to again. The pyramid is a whole new problem we must combat. So, let's crush them now and be done." Said the Wizard

"How shall you be hailed Wizard?"

"My name is Galant [pronounce GA lant]."

"Is there anything else we should know about this pyramid or beasts?" I asked

"Yes plenty: first, the pyramid is beyond my comprehension. It attacks with speed and fires at will meaning we cannot calculate its intensions besides to harm. Next, their troops are wild and mischievous. I have seen, as entering camp, your explosions and I do not think they have expected that, nor did I, and that is a great advantage. I can cast balls of fire, but nothing such as this. We'll have to talk further about how you managed all that. That is my summation at this point. I guess you are the one in charge, then?" Said Galant

"Oh, this is our Champion my friend." Out spoke Lisa [I wish she would get over that champion-thing and she wields it with unspoken humor, as usual.]

"Tonight, I want a recon party to pull back a couple of their dead to get a better look at them and look them and their possible weaknesses – maybe how they communicate. There has got to be weaknesses that we can exploit. Right now, we need to better manage every advantage to mess with. We had a victory today, but nothing like we need to be victorious. The real victory will be by downing the pyramid. Let's get cracking. We will raise another flag to call another meeting later today, so watch for it. I will need our numbers again, as well. Set outposts again for any raids and especially for movement of the pyramid. Now, Wizard Galant, can we expect any further re-enforcements? We need all the help we can muster. And please anything that comes to mind, our smarts are our aid." I asked

"Why yes as a matter of fact. They will come to follow. There is a witch, Witch Helga to be followed by another 5,000 troops.

Her benefactor is everyone, I mean to say, she will gladly help anyone, to the best of my knowledge with our cause, since she has lost thousands of countrymen to our enemy. Kill them or be dead is our moto." Said Galant

"Is there any preparations we should make right now?" Steve inquired

The wizard expands "Nothing more than making those explosives. That is awesome. I have the ability to hide my presence, but have never seen such force before. Where did that come from?" He queried

"It was just an idea. We have willing and able men that are working around the clock. Before you ask what a clock is, it means all of the time. Our next trick is to keep that pyramid from killing us in multitudes. I do not know what that trick is yet, unless you have an idea." I responded

"No, besides a pyramid cannot cross water but we are far from water. The ocean is 5 miles from here." Stated Wizard Galant

"OK, so there is something about water. I want to send out scouts to find water since that will give us a safer means to retreat. The water will also give us a tactical advantage for attacks. Next, we need reeds and ropes to keep this thing down during our attacks, if it is possible. I haven't worked that out quite yet. I want to tie it down, anchor it somehow. That even sounds stupid coming out of my mouth. Ignore that like you would your little sister if she wants some. Yeah, never mind, that is never going to work, it is a freaking spaceship. We need a report on the water. It is probably out of reach." I command

"Has anyone seen Amelia or Stacy?" Asked Steve

Lisa wrote this down and asked "Where are the dumb-asses?"

"They are contributing to morale of the men." I responded "Being serviced by the men and doing as little harm as possible; my idea. The guys love the attention, as do they."

"Nice, smart, keep them out of the way. I hope they don't get pregnant." Lisa responded

I said "Yes, could you imagine additional reprobates? Just think of the mockery of that."

[Witch Helga enters camp. Her hair is flowing black, long and beautiful. Nothing like the pictures you would imagine. I have only seen witches in movies and this is a huge fault of the industry. Although, should I be alarmed since any beautiful witch is normally evil with only an enchantment of beauty. I'll watch. I arrange a sit-down with her and the Wizard.]

"I am called Jeffrey, the Champion of this land, and I need information. Is there anything you have to offer in the way of knowledge about this pyramid and beasts."

She said "I carry a magical eye that sees what we cannot. And there is something about me, even when I am not using magic, that interferes with the vision of the pyramid."

"My God Jeffrey, she is beautiful and sleek; kind of mysterious as well. She will be regarded as a 'hands-free zone,' at my request." Whispered Lisa

Steve said "Yeah, and be cautious of her magic."

"This should be good. You can see the fear of possibly losing Jeffrey in Lisa's eyes. What will be down on this catfight? Amelia inquired "Shit, my money is on Lisa, magic or not. She is fierce. I have seen her fight like an Amazon chick. She might even be an Amazon. Just look at her legs. And how did she learn to wield a sword in the first place—like that? Odds? 3:1 in favor of the witch, agreed? Stacy insisted

"Agreed." Said Amelia

"Done." Says Stacy "But throw in a new horse?"

I spoke to Lisa "I think the pyramid is made of gold. Gold is Au for Aurum, Latin for gold and Au is imprinted on its doorway. Copper is much less dense and will melt at 2,000° versus 5,500°F like gold – I did very well in chemistry. Copper would have dented and bent more with the blasts like I was hoping. So, I am wondering next, why would the Golden Eye of Helga effect the pyramid's sight. I really don't care right now other than it does, and that is a help. Plus column. What is next then? The witch was also wearing golden wristbands. Does this also contribute, I wonder? Gold shouldn't matter, if the whole thing is gold. If we use the golden eye to observe, the gold wristbands to blind in addition to our sunlight, the fighters, the catapults, the re-enforcements, and attack again at dawn with the sun at our backs, our chance for fierce tenacity will increase marginally. Would that be enough? Let's try. That is all we can do is try, no matter the opponent."

I ordered "Get ready for another morning raid. Our odds are quite more substantial. Let's keep pounding them!" I want the same flankers to supply our catapults with fierce tenacity also and flanking positions. This time, I want to lead with the archers. They will be out front and try their hands at long-distance shooting to break their back before we get there. Before, they were scattered among the troops. The catapults have to be in place first. We should have 20 catapults now and a ton of black powder. Let's get moving."

"Fierce tenacity?" Lisa asked

I admitted "I heard it once, but was never able to use it in a sentence until now."

"You really need to get out more. I will teach you some phrases, like do me first."

[The archers shot first since they are rather silent. Then the catapults launched their barrage of rocks and explosives. There were explosions all over the enemy ground with shredded cats and earth being ignited into the air killing hundreds. There were buckets of rocks being launched and coming down like cannonballs. The pyramid does not take off at first. Is this because of the gold, even in the smallest amounts like the witch is wearing I wonder? What if they both affect it and what if they want to hoard the gold? We completed our task and retreated before the pyramid began to rise. While the ship was still down, I ordered the men to charge. They were slashing, stabbing, arrows flying while taking on these beasts. Then many woke and rebutted with their claws, fangs, and swinging their tails. They were a horrid enemy. We defeated the ones that woke and killed many of the ones still sleeping. I decided to retreat as we had our fill of good fortune for one day. I was exhausted being up most of the night staging this battle. I just need sleep again like Lisa assured me. So, I dropped like a failed farmer from the top of a barn. Maybe they need time to start their ship up and move?]

[I woke up and there where a circle of 'the Council' surrounding me. We all laughed.] "Yur were snoring, laughing und out uf yur mind sur, we ull had a gud yuk of it – no disrespect intended."

General McKellen offered up "Unly fur yur entertainment general." So wur r we?"

"Champion, everyone is in agreement that we delivered quite a blow to them this morning. I think we achieved the fierce tenacity you keep talking about. We have a chart as of 1 hour ago." Lisa reported "I took the liberty of arranging everything for your review Champion. They are as follows:"

Leaders	Ttl. Troops	Soldiers	Archers	Cavalry
Devlin	2,000	1,275	425	300
McGavin	475	300	50	125
Glen	300	200	50	50
McKellen	2,200	1,500	400	300
Wizard Galant	5,000	2,000	1,000	2,000
Witch Helga	5,000	2,000	2,000	1,000
Totals	17,775	7,275	3,925	3,575

I rounded some up by a few but minimally."

"Excellent, as this will save considerable time in reports. Do we have any reports on their numbers? They have been taking a beating, but I have a feeling that they too are getting re-enforcements from somewhere. During the night, I would imagine, so Steve, have more outpost reports. How are the manufacturing of catapults coming along? We need to make them non-stop as well as the black powder. Thank you, everyone." I instructed

"We have built 5 more and lots of black powder just overnight." Reported Steve

Glen said "Here comes some more of my lads. I have an extra 100 soldiers and 200 cavalries now they have arrived."

[Then, a group of 1,000 beasts worked their way behind us for an attack. This was a clandestine attack, they were on-the-hunt. Archers took out many, then cavalry and swords and spears. There was blood, red and black, everywhere. The men came running back to fight. Their fangs bit necks in half and their claws thrashed others. After a while, we put down the attack with our new numbers. It turned out to be only 14 deaths and mostly injuries. They were bandaged up and came back out to guard.]

"Witch Helga. I wish to use the Seeing Eye to spy on our enemy before each battle. This way, we will have intel about their state of readiness before we commit to battle." I spoke

"Then let's prepare another attack – they will not be expecting that since our two raids. I want to wipe out any remaining foot soldiers they have as quickly as possible. Are there any tricks that you have Wizard Galant or Witch Helga?" I inquired

[He takes me to speak in private.] "Yes one, but it is not really for any attacks. It is called a 'Back Rock' that once activated it will take you back to where you wish. It only works for a few people, usually 2 and sometimes 3 at most, depending on the honor of the one using it. It will then return you in a couple of hours or you may specify time." Said Galant

"I have a clock that tells time. I do not know of any others." Witch Helga reported

"Yes, we all have time pieces that actually fit on our wrist." Said Stacy, "That is when I know it's 'Last Call' and I can order 5 beers."

"Yes Helga, my 5 all have time pieces, so we can better co-ordinate any attacks and meetings and so on. We need to all synchronize our clocks accordingly." I directed

"We should also need a supply of Mead and beef, and Scotch for us, to celebrate today's victory with. Let's assemble the troops and decimate some killers! This time I want a flanking attack on both sides. If nothing else, it will be easier to retreat from. Be aware when using the catapults to cover our retreat that we will have men on either side of the direct attack, so we do not inflict danger or death on either side." I commanded

"Your will, be done, Champion." Said Lisa

[I take Lisa with me for her keen eye. We picked out a ridge from which to observe. Hopefully, we can identify any weaknesses during daylight with the sun to guard us. They are just lying dormant again waiting to be harmed. The wizard appears with a telescope. While the Seeing Eye will give us a small, focused picture, I want to see the full picture from an elevation. We are able to get a more accurate count and they have additions.]

"Maybe this will help. I also have an invisible cloak that may assist you. I have no need for it since I can pass undetectable. Take them. I did not want anyone else to know I have them since I do not trust anyone else – especially Helga, just yet. We will have to watch that one." Wizard Galant offered

"She did offer up gifts, so that is a step in the right direction." I returned

He said "Yes, but witches don't do that. When she offers up gold, snatch it up. That is when we know we can trust her, when she parts with them. They hoard, and I am willing to bet, so does she."

"I agree. Witches are greedy and thirst for more. You are wise Wizard." I stated

"Galant, I am glad you are with us, I have a good feeling about you. I already trust you and I think you are wise and bring good fortune. This is the beginning of a great friendship and a partnership that will last forever. I feel security when you are near."

"I feel the same way about you and I have a trained eye. You lead with honor and respect. I approve of everything you do and think. You are the reason these men are not dead already. Keep being the leader you are and we may just win this."

[I looked into the seeing eye. It showed vast destruction and chaos. It seems we have had a great victory, if I am seeing this right, it is blurry for me. I peer through the telescope and I see another 8-9-10 ogres. And more cats. Maybe I was wrong. Where did they come from, especially without any report? It seems that General Devlin's outpost no longer exists. Ogres begin their attack on our troops throwing massive rocks. The archers are taking them down; however, it takes time to kill a monster that size. Finally, they start to fall as do many of the foot soldiers. Lisa turns my head and indicates the pyramid is lifting off again. I do not what it is planning, but we have to push on.]

[Okay, launch the attacks. The catapults, now 15, have much more the effects as they hurl our bombs and smaller rocks like an old blunderbuss blast at the opponents. There is fire all over the battlefield. The catapults stop as our troops get close to their attacking positions. They attack again catches them off guard. The men attack swiftly and ferociously once more, especially cavalry. Throws of piercing spear, the thumps as giant spears stick, the slashing wings of swords in a cloud of dust and mayhem. Cats were dropping quicker than the men were. They leaped up at the calvary yanking them off, the swings of their tails cutting horses' legs. Maybe next time we could lure them into a trap.]

"Okay, sound retreat. Right now. Call back the men as we have few losses. I do not know where the pyramid went, but it is due back. Next, call in our outposts for now. I cannot leave more soldiers out there for fresh meat until I figure out how they killed our last outposts. For now, we have another victory to celebrate." I commanded

"Listen so I may be heard. Thank you everyone for doing such fine work. Our losses were one to their four, excellent work! I could see your determination. That victory was do to you all and all of your efforts. Be proud of yourselves for you have earned it."

[The victory dance begins. The scotch flowed like water. I had some weed still in my pocket from when I was whisked away. Lisa gets me to dance, but I warned her I cannot even dance like in college. I was really bad then and even worse now. There were a few minstrels with the English army. We still laughed, although the laughter is mainly jeered at me, I'm sure. We lay down under the stars and I asked her what's on her mind.]

She said "I had lots of questions like if things would have been different between us. How things could be now? Would we have kids and grandchildren now?"

I said "Everything has its purpose. Like you; I don't know what would happen to me or us without you right now. Even in your broken state of old age. I would be lost without you; you are so magnificent. You are the only sanity I have." I offered [I hugged her and we kissed deeply, and passionately.]

"You know that is the perfect kiss of the entire 6th Century and that would not have happened without you, right? I really needed that and that was a gift that may never have happened. Credit yourself with that for starters. Better you than Stacy or Amelia by far. Actually, I would never kiss those wenches anyway and I would be left yearning for a woman who is as passionate as you. How would you feel about that? Me walking around with my tongue hanging out; a dreadful sight for a Champion, right?" I asked

"Yeah, I would have to vote for another Champion." She laughed

"Let's get some shut-eye, my Championess." [We bed down as she kisses me goodnight.]

"Maybe for your protection, we should sleep together." I stammered

"Yeah, I have been getting cold at nights, too." She added

"Well, alrighty then. I get really warm while sleeping, so snuggle up if you get cold."

"I would enjoy that; you feel so right for me. And, I'll look after you." Lisa revealed

"I said you make me so happy and it is just natural for you. It is all you. You know, I do not think I ever stopped loving you after all of these years. I never thought we would see each other again, that was a sour feeling. I doubted myself for not telling you back then how I felt. Then there was my drinking getting in the way again. And here we are, just as destiny would have it. Reunited and for all of the right reasons. It only took one glance and you took my heart again. You are so beautiful, and quite a fine woman, I feel blessed even knowing you. I am liking this all over. I wish this was in another scenario though."

"Thank you, Jeffrey. You know, I understand exactly how you feel as I do feel the same. I would never have guessed that something so perfect could happen to me. I feel blessed. I keep thanking God in my prayers for you. You are just so special and caring about everything, everybody. I mean, who does this? I never met anybody like you."

"Just a moment and we can get back to us."

"Steve, send out some outposts except double them and only send out sober men. We may be fighting retribution for today's attacks. And try to keep the girls from getting pregnant overnight. Give them a responsibility like guard duty or tending to the horses for the night only don't make the mistake of counting on them. Thanks, Steve." I ordered

"We do not have any sober men. Not anymore." Steve responded

"Your wishes will be carried out, my Champion. I will find them. Looks like some of us are comfier than others." Steve commented

Lisa turns to me and chuckles "Do you think he is jealous?"

"I don't care as long as we are safe and comfy." I said "Stay fast wench." We chuckled

[Morning rolls in with fog and screeches from afar.] "I guess the men enjoyed last night as not many have stirred." I said "With this fog, I don't want to risk a battle without sunlight, or we would use twice the black powder to light our way and blind them. I think they will see better in this fog than us. And those screeches, dows that mean the pyramid has awoken? Let's see what the weather brings us. Any predictions Wizard?"

"You can expect fog and rain all day." Said the Wizard

"Quickly ensure the black powder is in the caves during this rainy mist of a day. Put everything on the outside of a ring and build a small fire in the middle to dry." I spoke

"Let's rest and add twice the numbers to manufacture with. Has anyone heard from NA – I mean Stacy and Amelia? There may be a problem with their behavior, well there is, but they are still under our care. The right thing to do is care for them as they cannot care for themselves. We need to keep doing the next right thing. It is like my Dogma. Besides, maybe they will grow on you; although probably more like a wart." I explained

Lisa adds "Or under you, more likely. They are always under foot unless you need them to accomplish something." She interjected "And their behavior grew into a migraine."

"Agreed, but for now we must tend to their care." I amplified

Lisa added "I am sure someone will tend to their care, upright or not, there will be an abled body about them."

"Jealous Lisa?" I question "Not hardly after last night," Lisa blurted out, laughingly

"Where are there sandy deposits or volcanos?" I asked

"There is lots of sandy ground around here, but why your request?" asked General Devlin

"We can make another weapon, called a magnate out of

minerals found both in volcanic rock and in the ground of sandy earth. We need both components since we do not have a lot of time to work with. I am sick and tired of losing lives and I think these can both help, well, they will help I believe. Let's muster *both* and we won't be losing time searching. Both have iron oxide to be magnetic. This won't be enough to affect gold, gold is not magnetic, but maybe their guidance systems will fail them." I added "This came to me as something was magnetic in the air last night and I dreamt of it. Let's get cracking right away."

"Yes Champion, I felt the electricity if that is what you meant." Lisa replied

"Oh, and later today, we will be taking a trip to try out this 'Back Rock.' We need a little trip to get away. I want to show you where I spent some time before I graduated. It is called Steamboat Springs in Colorado. It was wonderful for the most part. There were some difficult time, but mostly partying and making friends. Ever heard of it?" I asked

"Yea, sounds beautiful. I can't wait." She responded "Oh, and here is your troop report. We have like over 5,000 more and clearly the field advantage with soldiers and cavalry. More troops came in during the night, a small army for Galant."

"Great, and thank you Lisa." I responded

Leaders	Ttl. Troops	Soldiers	Archers	Cavalry	ogres
Devlin	1,600	875	425	300	
McGavin	525	400	25	100	
Glen	500	300	0	200	
McKellen	2,200	1,700	400	100	
Wizard Galant	7,000	4,000	1,000	2,000	
Witch Helga	5,500	2,500	2,000	1,000	
Totals	17,325	9,775	3,850	3,700	
enemy	14,505	14,500	0	0	5

"It looks like they doubled their strength." I stated "Nobody seems to know how they are getting reinforcements, but they agree that they are by the troop reports. Someone reported seeing another bright light in the sky, but thought that was the same pyramid."

"No one reported that to me." I said "So, there is a second pyramid bringing in reinforcements? Is that all. That really sucks and it was not reported to me!?"

Oh, quit whining like a little bitch. I will get someone Midol." Lisa said

"Well, it's only fair since we have been greatly reinforced Champion." The Wizard joked "We did have reinforcements and never even bothered to announce that to the opponents. Rather rude behavior, not very neighborly I would say, Champion."

"Home field advantage ought to help somehow." I stated

I said "Alright, have your jokes. The point is that I should have been notified about another possible light in the sky when there was a pyramid on the ground too."

[Galant gave me some gold and said it was for travel money. The trip goes great. We arrived instantly after my command: 'Back Rock, we wish to go to Steamboat Springs, Colorado, USA. There will be 2 people to travel and wish to stay for 3 hours. Move on.' I rented a car, although I do not believe they were ever paid in gold before. We traded the gold for cash when we arrived. I showed her Old Town and the resort, where I went to school and even the ski mountain up close. The moon is peaking over the mountain and it is time for another kiss. Then we are whooshed back without warning. Good thing I had my shorts back up. The funny thing is that it is like we never left. All the people and animals are in their same spots as when we left. We can use that to our advantage, too.

Now it's time to try out the 'Invisibility Cloak.' Lisa and I wrap it around us and vanished. We walked down to their camp and take a look around. They are mainly sleeping, with some prowling/walking around. I looked at the pyramid, but am afraid to touch it – I don't want to give us away. We grabbed some weapons and took them with us.]

I said "Come on, there is nothing more here to see."

[On the way back, Lisa asks if I saw those hideous beasts? I said I did and they looked quite ferocious. What about those strange men, all jittery-like? They were human-like but extremely frantic. That is who's weapons we took.]

I said "Come on, we have to hurry."

Lisa asked "Why do we have to hurry, are they waking up?"

I replied "No, did you not see me light that stick of dynamite under the one corner of the pyramid? I wanted to test its durability."

"Yes, I noticed; how could I not?"

I asked "Does everything stink to you? Besides that, they are big and ferocious-looking, tough and mean. If we didn't have the weapons we have, I wouldn't want to meet them on a battlefield. We'll take another day off tomorrow to amass more weapons and ammunition. Okay? Maybe blow some more shit up."

"Sounds good to me." Lisa returned

"I think another party is in order tonight; they deserve it. We should have it early though, so the men are fresh tomorrow." I said

"OK, sounds like a plan." Lisa said "Do you think we'll make it through this?" Lisa asked

"I will, God said; but he has not decided on your fate. Personally, yes, somehow, but I am not sure how quite yet. I know, the mighty Champion will rescue you!" I answered

Lisa said "Good, I'm glad you think so because I have my doubts."

[I hugged her with reassurance.]

"Just bad feelings, that I often get, about these things." Lisa stated

"By the way, Lisa, could you get counts on the black powder, catapults, and ore? We have to know where we stand all of the time." I asked "Sure Champion." She replied

Weapons	Black Powder	Catapults	Oil	Ore
Totals	25 lbs.	20	50 gal.	25 lbs.

"That was really quick!" I stated

"Well, it was already done and I just had to get it." Lisa responded

"Thank you, Lisa. That is outstanding, keep up the good work." I interjected

Devlin reported "We found this black gel-like substance while we were out chopping wood for catapults."

"Man, you have struck oil! We can use that. Great find!"

[I took Lisa down to a bathing hole the men have been talking about. With the men drinking, they will not be thinking about us and they'll be right by the kegs.]

"Lisa, what do you think about our witch?" I asked

"Well, I don't think she is very trustworthy. I know she has given us things, but that doesn't prove anything. Are there such things as good witches besides the Wizard of Oz?"

"Right." I said "I am afraid to use the mirror because it may snatch us up, imprison us or worse. Let's give this one time to prove herself." I added

[We started splashing each other and then I kissed her. Just as exciting and pleasant as before. So exciting, I fell tingly all over. She revealed she was swooned.]

"I think we really have something special here." I announced

[She agrees and nods her head. We laid down in the grass and explored our relationship further. It was like a dream come true. We went back after an hour of playing.]

[The next morning, I held another Council Meeting.] "Come to order. Today we are going to be digging ditches gentlemen. I want 3 ditches each 20 feet apart, 1 foot deep and half a mile long. I am hoping that our magnets will interfere with their maneuverability while the pyramid is flying. So, distribute the ore evenly in the ditches, reserving every third one for oil. We will dig on the hilltop above their camp out of sight. I know that is a lot of digging so let's get started. I want everybody on it, so complete the catapults started and everybody digs except the guards. Remind them to keep their weapons with them at all times. I do not think we are going to run into any neurosurgeons around here." I stated

[They attacked that night. We had reports of them coming, so we were ready for the fight. We cut loose the archers and the catapults first when they were 100 yards away. I had 50 archers on the side of the hill who were in-range. So, we were fighting from two fronts. Then the flankers charged in on the other side and hit them brutally. Our front lines attacked next and the coordinated effort paid off tremendously. The battle is successful, they had many losses. We learned that the magnetic ore does have an effect on disabling the ship; however, it effects their guidance system. The pyramid spun out of control like a car hitting an ice patch in a cartoon, but only for a minute. We need much more ore to have the drastic affects I was hoping for, I believe, however.]

"Steve, protect our trenches with catapults, but try not to hit them of course. Generals, get us more ore and ammunition – concentrate on that." I commanded

"Wizard, try to find some gold of our own. We can see if that has any bearing on the pyramid. If nothing else, we can use it as projectiles." I asked of him

"I know where, we had been here previously mining for gold." Galant said

Helga has a fit yelling "If you are going to throw it away, then I want it!"

"We will split it up evenly amongst us after it is all said and done if Galant okays it. Agreed?" I said [Galant nods yes]

"Yes agreed." They all stated

"We have a payday coming, I can get down with that." said Steve [Galant said he would get more gold for payment, as a gift from him.]

"The most important thing is that we win this thing first." I commented

"How do you win second, lose the win?" Lisa asked while laughing in her jest

"No, don't show up." I spoke

"Gold?" Asked Amelia "I love gold anything, the more, the merrier."

"They are here to either destroy us or we have something they want. I don't think they are just here to destroy us or they would just all-out attack." I offered "It may be that they think we have gold and they need it to make repairs to their ship. Afterall, we were thinking of gold before we were *dumped* here – no offense Generals, dropped." I stated

Stacy said "Maybe, if we can find gold, they will leave us alone."

"I kind of doubt that too. They will probably just want more and torture us until then. They'll probably attack to the end." I thought aloud

"What is the cave for?" Inquired General Glen

"It is for a flanking force to hide in until they have passed and then we'll attack them from behind." I explained "Let's get going then, unless there are any more questions."

"What else can we do then?" Lisa asked "There must be more that we can do." She added

"I honestly am out of ideas. More will come to us – patience is a virtue."

"So, what destroys gold?" Lisa asked

"Only a Fusion Reactor, that I know of." I replied "And I don't have one nor can we make one around here. Or a bigger piece of gold." I added

"We've got one at the university. Back in Pennsylvania..." Lisa sighed

"Wait; how big is it?" I inquired

Lisa responded "In my lab? They are small – a little bigger than the size of a rifle. We are developing them for the military, so I can get one. I am the Lab Director of Fusion."

"You see why I love you Lisa? Like I said before, you are very smart and resourceful."

"That's not all you said. Come on I want to hear it." She played

"Okay, you are drop-dead gorgeous." I added

"Are you thinking what I am thinking? We could use the 'Back Rock' to retrieve one." I suggested "Can we get one tonight? I asked

"Yeah, in fact that would work better." Lisa replied "There is a lot less eyes and questions that way."

"Well, then let's go." I spoke

[Lisa had to use the back rock since she had been there before and not me. Lisa showed me the Fusion Reactor and it is really cool; right out of Star Trek or something. The lab door opens and it is security. They request documents, but Lisa hasn't had time to complete them yet. There is a big hassle but she gets it straight. Then we are pulled back to camp, but way early. Thankfully, she had the fusion reactor in her hands.]

"Were you expecting to come back this early?" Lisa inquired

"No. it's not a problem this time, but might be in the future, so help me remember that please. We could be making love, pulled back, and found naked on the ground. What an embarrassing turn of events that sight would be, no warning, just there." I replied

Lisa said "Maybe we should try our luck. If we get caught, we could keep the tips."

[Camp is just as it was again, same timeframe. Everyone is eating and partying. I want to see my Council immediately to show them our new toy. I demonstrated one shot and it is awesome. Everything in its path is destroyed; right through the side of a mountain.]

"We will be using this in the morning. I want to set it up on the ridge above their camp tonight. I am hoping this will penetrate the pyramid. We will set up the catapults as usual. The men will hang back on the ridge until we are done firing. If you have any questions, ask now because once we hit the ridge, all quiet."

"Yes champion, understood." They agreed

Steve asked "Where did we get this; I never saw one before?"

Lisa said "At the university where I work – or did work until I took this. There will be hell to pay. So, I am back on the market boys."

"Okay, I'll take two. Lisa, how many shots does it fire in total?" I asked

"About 100 – 125 short bursts or 5 minutes in one giant spraying burst." She replied "And the great thing about these is that the particle beam also contains radioactive scavengers like nanobots that neutralize the radioactive isotopes to diminish any dangers to us after fired. That part has already been tested and it works. I don't know about the rest of it."

"We have a fusion reactor we are not sure about how or if it works?" I asked with a sigh

"Generals, have your men bed down early tonight and no more drinking as of immediately for our scheduled night time maneuvers." I commanded

[That night/morning at 4 am, we got a report that the beasts are forming for an attack. We were just about to begin to move the catapults when the beasts ran up over the ridge.] "We are under attack!" I yelled "Ready the catapults! Fire the catapults at will!" [The dark sky in which they love is now blinding them with explosions all around them.]

"Get your men into formations." I yelled

[We are caught off guard again with the outposts have already been taken out. The pyramid followed, but the Fusion Reactor is not ready to fire. It is still hidden in my tent. Luckily, we have already stationed 500 troops in the cave to attack from behind – this is another surprise for the sneaky beasts to gnaw on. They begin their attack as we attack from the front. We definitely catch them off guard from behind splitting their troops.

I came back with the reactor and begin to take aim when the pyramid blinds my sight. I call for Steve to take over and for Lisa to show him how to fire it. By this time, the pyramid begins to retreat out of sight.]

"Keep firing and follow them as far as the ridge." I commanded

[We linked up with our flanking force and I tell them not to go back to the cave; they'll be expecting that next time. But the flanking really worked this time around.]

"We are going to postpone this morning's raid to prepare more ammunition. Wizard Galant, station 1,000 cavalry on the ridge right up there on the right for a new flanking force. Witch Helga, station 500 cavalry in the land off to the left, north, to flank from that side. Wait for their forces to come through about halfway and start your attacks. Make more ammunition, not catapults. I also want more oil and to fill our trenches in case of another raid tonight. Have our outposts build fires tonight. I think the beasts can see better at night than we can. Also, that will give us a way to ignite the trenches if need be. That will blind them temporarily if they attack and definitely fry them.

We will be attacking at dawn tomorrow, so no partying and early to bed tonight." I ordered

"They have lightning bolts and now so do we, except Lisa's is far superior, we will be victorious!" I yelled

"What is a Humv?" Glenn asked

"You guys ask too many questions. It is a cart that you drive." Steve responded reluctantly

[At dawn, it looks like a beautiful day with few clouds and no rain. The flowers are in full bloom and I can hear the birds singing. It's time. Then, reinforcements came pouring out of the pyramid, thousands. The catapults begin to fire with explosions everywhere around the pyramid. We fire the Fusion Reactor 5 times with 5 direct hits - it hits whatever you aim at no matter how far away (like a laser, which it actually is). Each hit pierces the pyramid. The inhuman beings and beasts heard us hitting the pyramid and began charging. They are on our infantry quick and having luck with kills. It looks like they were re-enforced during the night because they now have over double on the attack. They now have enough to overrun us in one swoop. Now, they are coming out of the forest and corridor, so we have little, valuable time to defend ourselves. Our soldiers had fallen back and are about to be hit. The flanking cavalries are on their heels and hitting them with any weapon they have. We fire another

5 shots from the reactor. Now, both sides are in a full brawl, fighting for superiority. Men are falling now, but so are their beasts. The pyramid spins as to fire but cannot. You can see sparks and fire inside the pyramid through the holes the laser made. Their troops start spinning in circles aimlessly. Finally, the pyramid implodes from the inside out. Their forces retreat.]

[Once the pyramid is destroyed, I am transported back home into my chair. There is no sign of anybody else – just me by my lonesome. Lisa is gone out of my life just as quickly as we were reunited. I don't even know what university we were at. Hopefully, she was able to take the Fusion Reactor with her to return it and not get into a world of trouble.

The next day there is a knock on the door. It is Steve. I give him a handshake and a hug.] "How did you find me?" I asked

"I got your address from your Dad last year, remember?" He inquired

[We recounted our adventured. It's fun to talk about now since we are no longer in danger. I was never expecting an adventure such as it was.]

"Have you seen Lisa since we were returned?" He asked

"No and I have no way to find her. I just know her name and she is not to be found on Facebook nor the internet. I do not even know what city we were in at the university."

"Why don't you use your Back Rock and just have it take you back to that university?" He questioned

"That's a great idea Steve. Steve is back to save me again." I cheered him

[So, I gave it a whirl. I am transported to a large room with lots of people wearing lab coats. It worked! I see Lisa in the corner with a bunch of lab technicians. She is explaining what had happened in the test run. She didn't sacrifice her job so we could be saved after all. They are all in awe that she had the courage to try out the reactor – from what I can hear. She spotted me and hugged me with a kiss to boot. We are at her university in Pennsylvania – I recognize their logo. She pulls me into the circle of techs.]

She introduced me: "This is my Champion. Jeffrey is his name. He is the one who inspired me to try out the reactor and was there every step of the way. We did everything *together*, and I mean everything." [They all laugh and begin to clap in admiration.] "Does anyone have any questions for Jeffrey as I am not sure how long he is going to be here for his visit. Ask away, this may be your only opportunity." Lisa stated

"Yes Jeffrey, why does Lisa refer to you as a champion?" One doctor asked

"I actually am a champion of a land far away, long ago. I

commanded over ten thousand troops, had 4 generals, a wizard, and a witch. We built catapults, black powder, and magnets using our ingenuity. We fought a force of beasts and a pyramid that I think is a space ship. If it wasn't for Lisa's inventiveness and resourcefulness, we would not have stood a chance and been decimated. Now, does anybody know where the Psych Ward is? I think they may be looking for me." I explained

"That is amazing! I never met anyone like you before; your stature. It seems like you were the right commander for the job." A tech admitted

"I am genuine; a genuine what, I do not know."

I said "Hey, don't forget about Lisa. She was at my side and my right-hand-girl every step of the way. She stood up to these ferocious saber-tooth tigers and fought like a warrior."

"Are you planning to join us here at Collegetown?" Another tech inquired

"I plan on moving here but I do not have a PhD or anything. I am a manager of people and hospitality; that's my career. You guys are way too smart for me. I am surprised you would include me in a conversation. I hope I do not bore you."

"Well, I for one enjoyed your conversation." Lisa said

"Right now, I am a writer. I am almost finished with one book and am writing another. The first book is about an understanding of alcohol as an educational tool. I must explain that unfortunately I am an alcoholic. Part 2 of the first book is an autobiography. It has not been completed as my days of interest have not concluded. The bio even includes back when I met Lisa at college. She has always meant a great deal to me. She was even my Big Sister in my fraternity days. The second book is about the adventure we just experienced fighting beasts and technology way beyond phenomenal that we were fortunate to even survive. I do not know how our adventures will treat us or where they may take us, but I have an open mind and will. I believe this may just be the beginning – intuition. Thank you all for all your hard work and dedication or thousands would have perished. Thank you from all of them. If they were here right now, they would thank you themselves. Without the fusion reactor we could not have destroyed the pyramid that commanded their troops, as well as their ship's weaponry that we could not defend ourselves." I responded

"You said something about black powder. How did you think of that as a weapon?" A doctor inquired

"I thought about things in our history that would benefit our dilemmas. In fact, all of my ideas to communicate, mentor, lead, and survive were based on history, and a little science fiction. Black powder has been around since ancient China, but

then I realized the pyramid was gold and could only melt at temperatures over 5,500°F. Other than temperature, I knew the other thing would be a fusion reactor. Lis said let's try this and here we are."

"Thank you all but I have things to tend to." I commented

"Like Lisa?" Another tech laughed

"Yea, just like that!" I exclaimed

[Lisa takes me into her office. We kiss passionately. We make love on her couch in her office. Afterwards, we cuddle for a while.] She turned to me and said "I thought I lost you. One minute you were there and the next, gone. Yesterday, I missed you, but when today rolled around I thought you were gone forever."

I spoke "I know and I couldn't find you on the internet or Facebook, just gone out of my life as quickly as we were reunited. I was terrified, but there is always fate and destiny. Thanks to Steve, he gave me the idea that I could tell the Back Rock your name and here I am in the flesh. Luckier than a 4-leaf clover in the hands of a drunk Irishman, I feel."

"So, you saw Steve?" She inquired

"Yea, he has had my address and found me. I shouldn't have left him since he came looking for me. But he knows how much you mean to me. In fact, I wouldn't be here if he didn't suggest how to. I would be drunk in sorrow and hopelessness. So, I guess you didn't get in too much trouble for stealing the reactor." I inquired

"No [she just laughs], this is funny. They gave me a promotion with full tenure. They said I acted like the tenacious scholar I am. They had their reactor tested without any recourse to them, since it wasn't here and my work proved to be successful. The school will take most of the credit. This way they can apply for more grants and the school will do what they please with the new funding."

"Well, at least you got your promotion and tenure; that is great!" I exclaimed

She said "So, what are your plans? I heard you say you may be moving up here. That would be grand. Please do. You could even live with me if you like."

"Yes, and not just that. I plan on marrying you, so I don't lose you again. [I kneeled before her.] Lisa, will you do me the honor of becoming my wife, my Championess?"

"Oh my God, yes, yes, yes I will." Lisa swooned

"We have enough gold to build your own lab. We just have to take the Back Rock back and collect it."

"I still have to work for now, but when we get the gold, I can turn in my resignation and we can do as we please. Are you sure we can get the gold?" She asked

"I will not underestimate the Wizard. He even said he would get us more as a gift and I believe that as well." I spoke

"So, is that what you want to do from here? It sounds like a great plan. There is so much to see and things to do, we will be busy."

"For some time now, I have been thinking about us, even before we were reunited. This is one goal that is worth all of my effort to accomplish. I guess I should have thought about something before I asked you to marry."

"What is that?"

"Are you my true love or is it Amelia?"

"You sneaky shit. I did think there was something to worry about. Like when am I going to get my engagement ring? Or"

"Shut up and kiss me you fool."

Lisa asked "So, do you think the thinking about gold and jewelry or the wagons or any of that mattered?"

"All just clutter made of my own devices. I was a little too micromanaging the happenings."

"Well, let's get started. Maybe we will run to supply our catapults with your wishes of fierce tenacity right into another adventure; all that matters is that you are with me. Do you think there will be more adventures to come?" Lisa asked

I explained "I think every day from here on out will be an adventure being with you. I love you so very much. That is an adventure all of its own, one full of joy."

Printed in the United States
by Baker & Taylor Publisher Services